Dedicated to SueBee and Wendy.

Thank you for loving this story, from the very beginning.

The lights have become a blanket of sorts. They wrap me in bright white warmth, a shield against the faces that stare, the eyes that follow my movement. I used to squint when they came on, would duck my head to avoid the glare. I stopped that habit when I saw the world behind the lights—a world I don't want to see.

Two years ago, our manager decided to kill the lights. Their intense glare was exposing too many flaws – cellulite and flab not holding up well under stark spotlight scrutiny. I appealed to his better judgment, on my knees in his office, my hand on his cock. And so, in my case, the lights still blaze to life, bringing warmth, attention, and a glare of denial that blurs this world and allows me to picture another.

Now, I step on the dark stage, the cheap plastic of my platforms cutting painfully into the tops of my toes, every step bringing a pinch of pain. I keep my eyes down, following the flecks of silver on the unforgiving stage, waiting, exhaling a breath in controlled anticipation, my abs tightening.

The lights come to life and I have almost four minutes to escape.

PART ONE

In case I die, call the cops on this asshole.

NATHAN

"Sir?"

He turns toward the front seat, the Maybach's interior dimly lighting the man's features. "Give me a minute. I'm thinking." He looks back at the building, the neon sign crooked across its side, the red glow painting the entire parking lot the color of blood. "You sure it's her?"

Drew nods. "I'm sure. She's a perfect match for her driver's license photo. Gorgeous girl."

He chews on the inside of his cheek, considering.

"You should go in. See her yourself."

"I don't know. Maybe we should just go back to Utah. Look at that waitress again."

"You hated the waitress."

"At least she had her clothes on." He presses on the window control, the dark tinted glass smoothly rolling up, the glow of the sign diminishing. "Let's go back to the hotel."

Flipping open the folder on his lap, he turns on the interior light, glancing down at the image staring out at him, framed by the Florida driver's license. Candace Tapers. Blonde hair and a bright smile that didn't match the seedy strip club they were leaving. He closes the folder, her smile haunting him from behind the leather portfolio.

A stripper. What the fuck had he gotten into?

CHAPTER 1

Six hours later

My flip-flops smack through the front door and I kick them off as soon as I cross the cheap metal threshold. I drop my purse on the round kitchen table and pull it open, my fingers diving inside and pulling out cash, folded, stinky dollar bills, their edges worn, skin limp. I flatten the bills on the table, stacking them as I count, praying fervently, that it will be enough. I need at least three hundred dollars. My fingers stop moving and I run out of bills. $112. I sigh, counting out an even hundred and putting it in my wallet to deposit in the bank.

A belch sounds from behind me and I tighten, stuffing the bills into my purse. I grab my jacket and glance over my shoulder. "Hey Dibs." I flash a smile at the overweight man who stands in the doorway, his hairy chest exposed, baggy grey pajama pants sagging underneath his large belly. "Didn't think you'd be up this late."

He doesn't respond, his eyes trailing over my sweatpants and t-shirt, a flicker of curiosity in his eyes. "Surprised you're just now getting back. It's almost five in the morning. You were babysitting?"

"Parents had a late night," I say, moving around him, swallowing a shudder at the stench of cigarette smoke and body odor.

"You know rent's due."

"I'll get it to you tomorrow. I'm going to the bank in the morning." I open the door to my room, and step inside, closing it quickly behind me, hoping that he won't press the issue, won't pound on the thin door. I feel the vibration of his footsteps, his heavy weight moving to

7

my door. There is a moment of pause, then the continuation of steps down the hall. I relax, gently locking the handle and dropping my purse on the floor.

My room reeks of Dibs, his musty smells contrasting with the sunny scents I try to flood the room with. He's definitely been in here, doing godknowswhat. I want to shower, need to stand under hot water and rinse off the smell of the club, one of strangers, heavy perfume, and smoke. But the thought of a chance meeting in the hall with only a towel between me and Dibs... I decide to skip the shower and undress, pulling on a long sleep shirt and soft pajama pants. I crawl into bed quietly, listening for sounds in the house, hoping for the drone of Dib's snoring, praying that my tired muscles will bring me to a quick sleep.

Sleep doesn't come. I stare at the wall for over an hour, trying to occupy my mind with anything but numbers. The low balance in my bank account. The high balance on my credit cards. My dismal credit score. At least tonight was a good night. I didn't do anything that makes me close my eyes in shame, or curl into a ball and weep into my pillow. I danced and flirted, nothing more, nothing less. My purse is lighter for it, but at least I can sleep guilt-free. Except I'm not. I'm lying in bed and watching dawn tickle the edges of my blinds, my stress keeping sleep at bay.

Poor Planning. If I ever have a book, that's going to be the title of it. I had a worry-free childhood that led to a diamond-studded high school career, which led to an I-don't-care-about-grades college experience, which concluded with a useless graduation ceremony and a useless degree proudly framed and promptly stuck into a cardboard box in my parents' garage. I celebrated my college graduation in high style, entering the Real World with a wallet full of fresh credit cards and a new profile on Monster.com. I was ready to find a job and live life as an adult.

One year later, I came to the conclusion that no one wants to hire an event planner with no experience, a questionable GPA, and no references, no matter how cute her Betsey Johnson dress is, or how knowledgeable she is about the local party scene. My credit cards were maxed out, I was three weeks late on my rent, and I was desperate. I worked at Best Buy for a few weeks, the job offer graciously offered by a drinking buddy, but the monthly income didn't come close to covering my credit card minimum payments. So I drove twenty minutes outside of town and stopped in the parking lot of Sammy's, a strip club located on the county line, and the only option for local men and drunk tourists.

That was three years ago, and I sat in the parking lot for forty-five minutes before I found the courage to walk in. Looking back, I wish I'd just driven off. Fuck the fact that it doubled my Best Buy income. Best Buy never led to blowjobs just before rent deadlines or married assholes trying to slip their fingers past my g-string.

I have no great excuses for how my life has turned out. It was a simple case of poor planning. Laziness. A year of living it up, courtesy of Capital One and Jennifer Garner's damn ads promising double miles.

I close my eyes, and sometime around dawn, sleep finally arrives.

CHAPTER 2

My rent's salvation walks through the front doors at 9 p.m. I am moving through tables, my eyes dancing over prospects, when a firm hand grips my elbow, hot pink nails digging into my skin. "Look alive, Candy. Rick's looking for you."

I glance back, carefully prying Jez's talons out of my arm. "Fuck Rick." Yes, *fuck* Rick and his suggestive offer of a double shift. My desperation must be showing, something I need to get a handle on, ASAP. If there is anything our boss loves, it's taking advantage of his harem in our times of need.

"Candy." Rick's voice cuts through the thump of the music and I roll my eyes, turning to face him.

"Yep?" I drawl, smiling for the benefit of the middle-aged man who passes, his eyes lingering across my gold-dusted cleavage.

"We've got a high-roller requesting you." He pulls at my arm, not allowing me an option, and I stumble forward, my heels catching as I hop and skip to keep up with him.

"What the hell? Slow down!" I hiss at him, narrowly missing the sharp edge of a table as he drags me along.

"The guy's up in VIP. He's waiting for you." Rick practically sprints forward, as if this "high roller" is moments away from disappearing. I fight the urge to laugh. The guy probably asked for sparkling water and Rick thought him fancy. Our club is an establishment for truckers and minivan driving tourist dads; anybody with any taste or money took their plane to New Orleans or Atlanta if they wanted high quality girls.

"I'm telling you, this guy is loaded. He already ordered a bottle of champagne—you know that bottle of Dom we keep in the back? Plus, he has private security and came in a *limo*." Rick practically pants with excitement, his mouth so close I can smell the hamburger he had for dinner, his hand still pulling me along,

I allow myself a speck of excitement. This guy *does* sound loaded. Maybe this night will be different. Maybe I will actually meet someone worthwhile, someone who doesn't try to haggle over the price of a lap dance, or who will try and cop a free feel. We round the corner and Rick pulls back the curtain that encloses the VIP section. He steps aside and I move forward and into the dimly-lit space.

It's hard to put a diamond in the garbage, but our VIP room is a gas station trash can and this man is a Harry Winston diamond. My eyes skip over the empty center stage, over the empty black couches, their cushions ripped and saggy, and hone in on the man.

He dominates a center couch, his back against the leather, his arms draped out like wings on a plane, a lit cigar glowing from his right hand. Behind the couch, two men stand, their features hidden by the shadows, their silhouetted builds impressive. *His security.* From the end of the cigar, smoke drifts, a smoky trail across the man's face, his smug smile widening as I approach. I take the final step, my heel dragging along the bumpy carpet before stopping. This close, I can see his eyes. Bright blue, vivid and turquoise, the sort that matches Caribbean waters and the neon glow of my bedside clock. Will I be staring at it tonight? Will this man ask something of me that will cause guilt-fueled-insomnia?

I mask my apprehension, holding my posture straight, tits out, stomach in, a smile across my face. "You asked for me?"

He brings the cigar to his lips, taking a slow drag on it, his eyes taking a slow and unapologetic tour down my body. I fight the urge to cross my arms over my chest. His eyes flit to the pole, then back to my face.

"Dance."

A one-word asshole. I almost prefer them, the type that issue orders and shut the hell up. Better them than the romancers, the ones who fawn over you while detailing updates about every part of their lives.

I nod, glancing at Rick, who steps back, toward the hall.

"I'll turn on the system and load your playlist." Rick does a ridiculous little forward bow toward the stranger, who ignores him, his eyes now trained on my face.

I shift my weight and clasp my hands behind me, my knuckles brushing against my ass, the Brazilian thong barely covering anything. I should have worn the sparkly back corset tonight, the set much nicer than this one—a bikini missing half of its sequins and faded from too many washes. "How's your night going?"

The only movement comes from the fingers of his right hand, the cigar rolling slightly.

I let out a breath and step back, turning to the stage. Fine. Fuck small talk. I can wait in the back of the stage until the music comes on. It can't take more than a minute, not with the haste Rick seems to be assigning to this jackass.

"Why are you doing this?" Five words that stop me, his tone one which doesn't allow for avoidance. I turn back to face him, the answer falling out quickly. "Student loans. Credit card debt."

I used to lie. It's the most common question from clients, followed closely by whether my breasts are real. I used to tell a detailed sob story about a sick mother and her medical bills. Clients ate it up and my G-string filled with their sweaty, sympathetic bills. Then my mom died. My dad got sick. Karma laughed, and I ditched the lies. They were unbelievable anyway. I can't even cover my own bills, much less contribute anything to my dad's care.

The man doesn't respond to my comment, his cigar lifting to his mouth, obscuring some of that beautiful face. There is a crackle of a speaker and then the lights come on, the spotlights cutting through the room, the barren stage now pooled in color. I turn, grateful for the distraction, and move quickly to the stairs, my steps growing more confident as I climb the wooden rungs and stride onto the stage, the first DMX beat hitting hard in the moment that I grab the cool metal pole and swing into the air.

Flying. A hundred hours of practice, and the action is seamless as my heels fly through the air, my momentum perfect, one leg hooking on the pole, my speed increasing as I spin once, twice, three times, my muscles tightening on the pole, my speed slowing in perfect cadence with the beat, and I release the final ounce of breath in the moment I land.

I am reckless on a pole, trusting my legs and arms in a way certain to cause damage. It is a lover I hate and I ride it relentlessly, caressing it in a sensual way that leaves nothing to the imagination. The beat moves through me and I get lost in its strength, pulsating against steel, spinning away only to return to it, my heels a blur of clear sparkle, my thoughts lost in the movement.

Everything is a swirl of bright lights, the dark back wall of the stage, the glossy black of the floor, the chrome of the pole. I can't see the stranger or those blue eyes, can't see the men who protect him, or the glow of his cigar, the five-o-clock shadow that had coated his jaw, or the dark clean lines of his suit.

My bra is the first victim. One quick unclasp, the release of heavy breasts as I spin slowly downward, my legs suspending my body upside down above the hard floor. One outward fling, and sparkles and black sequins become airborne and joyful in their flight. I keep my panties on, the thin fabric the only thing between me and the pole.

When the final beat hits, I am panting, my back against the pole, my legs trembling slightly from the performance. The lights flicker off and my eyes move, traveling across the empty room and over to his. The eye contact is terrifying, the cigar tight in his mouth, a fierce look in his eyes. It is more than simple arousal, a hungry and possessive stare that rips pieces of me off and marks them as his, each dagger of eye contact laced with blatant desire that he makes no attempt to hide.

"Come here," he commands.

I move carefully down the stage's steps, my sky-high stilettos wobbling slightly on their downward descent. Then I am before him, watching as his hand moves, adjusting himself, the hard line of his cock outlined in his pants. He glances down at it, then at me. "Suck me off."

I hesitate, the look in his eyes intoxicating, a vivid blue that commands. Against my tongue, the questions formulate. *How much?*

What about your security? I swallow the questions, along with the sentences that I typically say. *I'm not a prostitute. How about a dance instead?* I don't want to dance for this man. I want, more than anything, to unzip his pants and wrap my lips around his cock. I want to feel the arousal, to know that it is all caused by me, to know that this beautiful wealthy man finds me attractive. Despite the shitty club, or my worn-out bikini. I fall to my knees, the carpet scratchy against my bare skin, another reminder that what I'm doing is wrong. I think whoever picked it out had us in mind, wanted every stripper in this place punished whenever we fell to our knees and broke the sacred rule that everyone in VIP loves to ignore.

My hands work the smooth leather of his belt, the zipper of his pants. I flick my eyes up, glancing behind him, where motionless and silent, the two bodyguards stand, their eyes forward and hands clasped. I look back to him, pulling apart the top of his dress pants. He is wearing thin boxer briefs, and I slide my hand into them, a hiss coming from his mouth when I wrap my grip around his cock.

"Your hands are cold. Just use your mouth." There is a slight break in his words, a catch in the vowel that gives me confidence, my eyes closing as I tilt the stiff length of him toward me and lower my mouth to his tip.

He's big in my mouth, my lips sliding over rock hard thickness. He groans and I place my hands on his thighs, working my mouth up and down his shaft, taking him as deep as I can manage before withdrawing, the sounds of the blowjob loud in the quiet room.

There is the creak of leather as he settles back against the couch, his thighs flexing under my palms. "Keep going." I do, my lips stretched around his thick length, his cock flexing against my tongue. Minutes pass, and then I feel his hands, firm on the back of my head, pulling himself deeper into my mouth. He growls and his cock twitches, his cum filling my mouth, his grip tilting back my head, his eyes capturing mine as he finishes, intense blue orbs of possession locked on me. Then his eyes close and his head drops back, his cock pumping one final release into my mouth.

I pull slowly off of him, moving backward on my knees, my attempt to stand uncoordinated, my left foot choosing an inopportune time to fall asleep. One of his bodyguards steps forward, helping me to my feet, a fold of crisp bills discreetly pressed into my palm. I don't know who he's hiding it from. There are only four of us in this room, and every one of us was an audience to what I just did.

I glance toward the man, who is sliding his belt into the clasp. He looks away, making eye contact with the other bodyguard. "Let's go."

Of all of tonight's words, those two cut the hardest. Even more than *suck me*. I feel cheap and used, the fat roll of cash burning at my palm, and if I was a stronger woman, I'd give the money back.

But I'm not a stronger woman. I'm a broke idiot of a girl who needs rent money and who has been in this same place a half dozen times before. At least most of the men thank me. Most ask for a hug, or a kiss, or at least fake kindness.

I watch them leave, and I am suddenly alone in the room. I open up my palm, my fingers slowly moving through the bills. A thousand dollars.

It doesn't seem like enough for my dignity.

CHAPTER 3

I leave a hundred dollars on the dining room table, along with a check for the rest of the rent. The house is dark, snores coming from Dibs room, and I step into the bathroom, turning on the shower and stripping in the middle of the tight spot.

I don't know what I expected. That he would pull me to my feet and onto his lap? That he would nuzzle my neck and plant kisses on my mouth, and ask me on a date? He was probably on I-10 right now, his limo headed somewhere else. Or on a private plane, the Destin airport just a stop in his flight plan. A short stop for gas. Something to eat. A blowjob and dance.

I test the water with my hand and step under the spray, pulling the curtain closed, the rings rattling against the rod. I close my eyes and take a deep breath, putting my face under the water. If only he hadn't been so beautiful. It's easier to forget the ugly assholes that leer while adjusting their beer gut. *This man* … I come up for air, wiping the water out of my eyes, my fingertips black from the mascara. This man had been painful in his perfection, his intensity only enhancing his fierce good looks. He is probably married. A father. He probably has some perfect model in a mansion sleeping on thousand-dollar sheets and waiting for his return. No way a man makes it to his age without being snatched up.

Not that it matters. He didn't come into Sammy's looking for a wife. He came into Sammy's looking for exactly what he got. I squeeze some face wash into my palm.

I think the issue is that I had liked it. I *liked* his cock in my mouth. I *liked* the look in his eyes when he watched me, the blatant need, as if

I had been special. My body had *responded* to him, to his stare, to his touch. At one point he had tugged gently on my hair, had trailed his finger across my shoulder, and my body had *ached* at the contact. I had wanted—no, I want more. I want him to come back in. I want to feel his hands on my body; to do more than cum inside my mouth.

This is the first time I've ever been attracted to a patron. I don't know if it's the mystery, the money, the perfect features, or the cock, but I *want* him.

I close my eyes and push my head underneath the water, holding my breath. Maybe I just need to get laid. Scott would do it. I could call his cell and he'd be rolling out of bed as soon as I said the words. Seven months since our breakup, and he was still persistently around.

I lean forward and twist the knob, the water dying. Nah. Ten minutes with Scott wouldn't solve anything. I'd still be thinking of this guy, and would have confused Scott even further.

I step from the shower and reach for my towel.

***

"Candy, you're up."

I look over my shoulder, raising an eyebrow at Dwayne, our bouncer. "Up?"

"That guy's back. He's asking for you again."

He's back. I bite my lip to hide my smile, turning back to my locker and stuffing my makeup bag inside.

"Good lord girl, you are lucky." Jezebel hisses, leaning against her locker, her eyes on her phone. "There's a *number* of things I'd like to do to that man."

Tell me about it. I shrug, like he isn't the best thing to walk through our doors in years, fighting the urge to bear my teeth and lay claim. "Can you take my spot? I'm supposed to dance after Mandi." *He asked for me.* Just like before. Where had he gotten my name? Had one of my regulars referred him? I thank Jez and close my locker, my mind running through all of my clients who may have … it's a dead end task. Strippers are like sports picks. Men love to brag about them, but when it comes to sharing details, they keep their mouths shut, uninterested in walking in and finding me grinding up against their friend.

I wind through tables and head to the VIP room, ducking through the velvet curtains, expecting to see him at his prior position, but the couches are empty and I am on full alert as I turn in a circle, searching the dim room. My shoulders relax silently when I see a group of men in the corner, Rick's large mass present. They turn at my entrance, Rick's face tinged with something akin to guilt. His hand moves quickly, and something disappears into his pocket. *Cash? Drugs?* Neither would surprise me. I fight to keep emotion off my face as my mind works hard at understanding what I am about to walk into.

"Candy," Rick steps forward, clasping my hands in his sweaty palms. I stare at our hands, then shoot him a glare that causes him to drop the connection, a quick nervous motion that only raises my guard more. He takes a deep breath. "Candy, this gentleman has requested you to join him. Outside the club, I mean." He flusters, wiping his sleeve across his forehead. "He wants you to go with him."

The words don't make sense. I take a moment, and look over Rick's cheap polyester shoulder and at the stranger. Tonight, a different suit, paired with a tie, and the look is almost groom-like in its formality. He stands, feet apart, hands loose in his pants pockets, a confident stance that matches the level gaze he delivers. "Leave? Alone?" I can't leave with him. It was bad enough what I did here, at the club. Leaving with a client … I swallow. Whatever I do in this building, at least I am safe, protected. Walk out the door with a client, and I might as well be a twenty-dollar Fort Walton hooker.

"My security will accompany us." The words come from the blue-eyed stranger who steps forward, stopping beside Rick. *His security?* What good will that do me?

"And where would you take me?" Two years ago, one of us disappeared. Cindy Swans. Three weeks later, her body floated up somewhere around Pensacola. That's the problem with living on an island. Give a man a boat and some concrete blocks, and you're one wrong comment away from disappearing.

"To my suite." His eyes meet mine, without hesitation, and if there was a pool to drown in, it'd be those murky blue depths. "The accommodations are very comfortable."

My heart rate increases, as my mind actually considers the possibility. *I can't leave.* There are a thousand reasons against it and only two reasons for it. Money is one, the ache between my legs another. This man wouldn't take me somewhere and be content with a fifteen minute blowjob. He'll want more. And right now, my hands trembling, body aching … so do I. *I shouldn't leave.* Last year, Bethany started escorting on the side, and ended up in a trailer in Defuniak Springs, addicted to meth and some asshole named Justin. That could be me—I could be one stupid decision away from that life. And *this* could be my stupid decision. This could be the "just one time" that becomes a gateway to prostitution. Arrest. A pimp who feeds me drugs and invites spring breakers to try me on for size. "When would I return?"

He grins slightly. "In the morning. My driver can return you to the club."

In the morning. A suite. A night spent away from Dibs and bills and my shitty life. I raise my chin slightly, keeping my eyes on him, and try to ignore our audience. "How much?"

His mouth twitches a little, and I can't tell if it's in disappointment or pleasure. "I'll leave that up to you."

I take a deep breath, my stomach churning with a mix of trepidation and excitement. "In that case, I'll grab my purse."

CHAPTER 4

My first night at Sammy's, I believed in fairytales. I thought there was a chance of ending up like Julia Roberts, just days from a dashing, dignified Richard-Gere-type whisking me away to a lifetime of diamonds, caviar, and True Love.

Now I understand the truth. In this hellhole, my best hope for a happily ever after is the Anna Nicole Smith Dream – that an old rich man will hobble in, decide to part with half his riches so his few remaining years will be filled with bouncing breasts, bubble baths, and blow jobs to celebrate mahjong wins. I am almost happy with that scenario, happy with a slice of the good life minus the love. Love seems to be set aside for those who deserve it, for those who plan ahead, those who recycle and donate a dollar to the March of Dimes at the supermarket register. I'm a non-donater. I'm the girl who spends that spare dollar on a candy bar instead. I don't deserve love. Ten years with a centenarian—that seems like a more attainable future.

We haven't had a rich old guy in quite some time. Coco came close to nabbing one, had a pasty white ancient who was all about her ethnic curves. But he died, mid-fuck, a heart attack yanking his life away as she rode up and down his scrawny body. His family was less than accommodating, kicking her out of his mansion with no ride home, and no invitation to the funeral.

This guy is too young to be my love story, too handsome, too perfect to have any part in the rest of my life. His type marries blue blood heiresses who keep their cardigans clean and their sex cleaner. This invitation to leave with him is not the start of a love story. It's just sex, in a location less public than our VIP couch. Sex for money, the amount seemingly up for discussion. With this man, I am willing to break my No Sex Rule, my body desperate for his touch – my bank account in bad need of a cash infusion. He'd paid a thousand dollars for a blow job. How much will he pay for an evening?

Our back room reeks of lotion and perfume. I open my locker and grab the worn Michael Kors bag—one purchased on a girl's trip to New York sophomore year, back when a new student loan replenished any shortage of funds, and credit card limits increased every time I asked. I check my phone, and grab a peppermint, twisting the plastic ties and popping the mint into my mouth.

"You going somewhere?" A South Carolina drawl coats the syllables, the accent one that can only belong to one person—Nikki.

I yank a bright blue minidress off a hanger and turn to the petite redhead, who grips an open SlimFast can and a half-eaten Milky Way bar.

"Leaving early." I work my arms into the dress and pull it over my head.

"With that guy?" Jealousy is never pretty, but on Nikki, it comes dipped in kerosene, with a blowtorch in hand. I won't be surprised, if the moment I turn my back, she dials the cops and turns me in for prostitution.

"He's an ex-boyfriend," I lie, and it's a moment of pure brilliance, her features falling in disappointment before her glittery lips slide back into a smile.

"Oh." She straightens. "He broke up with you?"

I sling my bag over one shoulder and slam the locker. "It's a long story. I'll tell you later."

I push past her before she can argue the lie.

***

My hand tightens on the strap of my purse as I come to a stop. The man turns away from the group and lifts a chin to me, his eyes flitting down my dress and then back to my face.

"You ready?"

"I'd like to take a photo of your driver's license." I practiced the words in my mind before I spoke, yet they still come out stiff and unsure, as if I am asking for something that is negotiable.

Even in the dim light, I can see the flicker in his eyes, the tightening of his chin, a subtle shift of his shoulders.

"That's not really—" The words, spoken by a beefy suit to our left, are cut off by just a glance from the stranger.

His eyes return to me, and a knot of tension in my chest relaxes a little when he reaches into his back pocket. "Smart girl," he says quietly.

Smart girl? I haven't been a smart girl for a very, very long time. A smart girl would run away from his delicious mouth and intoxicating scent. A smart girl wouldn't be trading cash for her safety and respectability. Still, a part of me preens at the empty compliment. It's been so long since a man has admired anything but my looks.

I reach out and take the driver's license he offers, examining it briefly before digging into my purse for my phone.

Nathan Dumont. An unsmiling photo that matches his handsome face. Born eight years before me, which puts him at 35 years old. An address in Nashville. A Tennessee man in our little beach town? *Random.*

I take a photo of the license, and text it to Jez, briefly depressed by the fact that my life has degraded to the point where my only friends are strippers. I add a quick message. *In case I die, call the cops on this asshole.* Sending the message, I pass the card back to the stranger, one now with a name—Nathan—and a location. I tuck my phone back in my purse. *Smart girl.* Maybe I am. Maybe somewhere, underneath the glitter and the desperation, there was still a little of the person I used to be.

CHAPTER 5

As a teen, I always pictured limos and strippers paired together—like peanut butter and jelly. Now, I step onto the parking lot in five-inch heels and try not to gawk at the stretch limo that idles, the door smoothly opened by his security detail. I stumble at the door's opening, trying to figure out the most ladylike way to get in while wearing a mini-dress. I end up doing some sort of dippy crawl that is a disaster, my face flushing as I right myself on the leather seat. The door closes and I have a moment of silence.

It's sad that I feel at home. The mirrored ceiling, with twinkling stars set into the headliner, is straight out of the low ceilings of Sammy's. The black leather seats, ice chest of beer and wine, a velvet pillow lying against the front seat – it's all Stripperville, USA. And for me, it's all incredible. High-class, fancy living, incredible. I am in a *limo*, with a wealthy stranger, pulling away from Sammy's. If I squint hard enough, this is just like Pretty Woman's final scene. Maybe I *can* be Julia Roberts. Maybe I *can* have a fairytale ending, despite my poor planning.

I shut down my fantasy when the other door opens, his tall body making an easy transition into the car, nothing like the fumbling giraffe I had been. I fix my mouth into an easy smile, crossing my legs and leaning forward, assuming the pose that makes my breasts appear biggest and causes my cellulite to disappear. "Where are we going?"

He ignores my question, unzipping his pants and leaning back in the seat. "Come here."

For such a smart girl, I'm an idiot. My fantasies scamper away, and I remind myself of my reality—one where I should count my blessings if I manage to survive the night. I keep my smile, and hope the disappointment doesn't shine through my eyes. I slide closer along the seat, and he nods toward the floor. "On your knees."

I almost say *please*, almost demand that he treat me with an ounce of respect. But I don't, and my first limo ride ends in the way that most stripper rides do. My head between his thighs, automotive carpet rough against my knees, his hand on my hair, pushing my head onto his cock. The car drives, I suck, and any excitement I have for the evening ends in his finish.

***

After his orgasm, there is only silence, an uncomfortable ten minutes where I look out the window and consider pulling out my phone. Would it be rude to fit in a level or two of Candy Crush?

He doesn't seem concerned about manners or small talk. As soon as he finished, he had zipped his pants, helped me back to my seat, and then gotten on his cell, his fingers busy across the screen, emails sent and replied in rapid succession. I curl my knees to my chest and lean against the cushion, watching the lights of Destin, then Santa Rosa Beach, then gulf-front homes, go by.

"Here." He holds out his jacket, covering my goose-bumped legs. "You look cold."

"Thank you." I tuck my hands in between my thighs and wonder where we are going. Maybe Panama City Beach, though they have their own strip clubs there. Chances are, if he came to Sammy's, we are probably almost there.

The limo slows in a bit of late-night traffic, and I watch the stark-white homes of Alys Beach, a neighborhood of the uber rich who all prefer cookie-cutter homes devoid of any color. I wonder what they do when they get drunk at their wine dinners and stumble home. Do they get lost in their mirrored maze of identical homes? During the spring, is their all-white landscape tinted yellow from the pollen?

Watercolor, then Seaside passes, the tiny communities filled with preppy teenagers on bikes, their Vineyard Vines polos bobbing through the crowded streets. I watch two girls perched on the hood of a Range Rover, cell phones in hand, the screen's glow lighting up sun-burnt young skin. I want to roll down the window and scream at them to all go home, to study, to appreciate the fact that life blessed them with fucking perfection. They'll never be in a polyester minidress and leopard-print hooker shoes, trading dignity for greasy bills.

I close my eyes and relax against the headrest.

NATHAN

These kids are assholes. Not that he can talk. Twenty years ago, he was stealing sips of bourbon in the fucking box at the Derby. Spending spring breaks in Kiawah, and fingering Stacy Hanover against the side of her dad's Ferrari on Christmas Eve.

His parents' death almost saved him, in the twisted cruel way that God worked. Their car accident cut off the cash flow, and made him realize exactly how quickly a trust fund could be depleted. He'd been practically broke when his sister had bailed him out, loaning him ten million dollars and believing in his vision of redeveloping a struggling neighborhood in Nashville. That loan, and her faith, had been the building blocks of Dumont Development, and the man he had become. Her investment, and her expectations, were the only things that had saved him from the future that waits for every one of these rich teenage pricks.

He looks away from a cluster of giggling teenagers and over to the tiny curl of a body, pressed against the limo's opposite door. She couldn't be farther from him, her position one that lights every protective fuse in his body. He turns away, his hands instinctively tightening into fists. He's not here to protect her. He's here to use her. And the sooner she understands that, the better.

CHAPTER 6

We end up in Rosemary Beach, at a fancy hotel where a valet opens my door and helps me out while staring at my legs. I clutch my purse to my chest as we ride up the elevator, this time with only one bodyguard beside us.

I lean toward Nathan and lower my voice. "Is the bodyguard staying in the hotel also?"

He glances up from the phone in his hand. "Does it matter?"

I shift, watching the numbers climb on the elevator's display. *Does it matter?* Probably not. He seems to be there to protect Nathan, not me. If anything, should a bad situation arise, it'd be better to fight off one man than two.

The elevator sounds, and the doors open. The bodyguard gestures me forward, and I step out.

"Stop." Nathan's word is a growled command and I instantly obey.

We are just inside the suite, a pale room decorated in blues and creams. The windows are dark, and in them, I see a small reflection of myself, a thin slice of vulnerability, framed by the two men. To my left, a large dining table. To my right, Nathan. I look to the table, and wonder if the tremble in my bones is visible to the men.

His hand touches my back, sliding my hair over, pulling the strapless minidress down, over my breasts. There is the light dig of his fingernails, and then the clasp of my swimsuit style top is undone.

I turn toward him, his eyes meeting mine as he reaches up and unties the strings around my neck, his fingers trailing over my skin as he pulls it away. I wet my lips, stalling. "We haven't discussed money."

"That didn't stop you from sucking my cock." He doesn't smile, and the first real stab of fear hits me.

I shiver in the cool air, feeling the fabric brush against my nipples as my top falls at my feet. "I don't normally do this," I whisper.

"What, leave the club?"

"No. Sex. That isn't something I do with clients." *And not something I am going to do for free.* My body argues with my mind, physically pulled to the man, my hands wanting to reach forward right now and take his cock into my palm. My mind understands the reality of my situation and pushes back, winning the fight.

His eyes are thousand-foot depths with flecks of blue domination in them, his tan skin stretching over perfect features as he speaks. "Ten grand."

I swallow as his hands slide down my sides, pushing the minidress lower. I feel a cheap stretch of fabric as he slides the polyester over my hips and then drops it to the floor. His fingertips, a little rough on their surface, trail back up, over the curve of my ass, and I feel them dip beneath the lace of my panties. *Ten thousand dollars.* A figure I can't turn down. Not that, at this stage in the game, turning him down is necessarily an option. "Okay." I'm not sure if I actually speak the words or just mouth them.

He yanks outward, the quick motion startling me, a ripping sound heard, and then I am naked, feeling a tickle of lace as the ruined cloth that was my panties drops to the ground between my heels, my eyes passing over his shoulder and colliding with the man who stands at attention, watching us.

"Your man," I whisper, feeling the strength of his hands as they move over my body, gentle and caressing, my breasts the current object of their focus. I am a woman conditioned to touch, conditioned to stolen gropes and caresses, some worshipful, some crude, all of which occur in the smoky air of Sammy's. Here, in a room that smells of ocean and money, with a man that reeks of class and power—every point of contact is magnified, my senses overwhelmed, my heart crying out for more.

Ten thousand dollars. I hope he is gentle. I hope he is kind. I hope, what is about to happen, isn't something that I will regret for the rest of my life.

His fingers spread, running lightly over my nipples, which stand to attention under his touch. "He stays."

"But…" my voice is as weak as my knees. "He can see us."

His hands still and he moves forward, so close that I have to tilt my face up to meet his. "That's the point. I thought you, of all people, wouldn't be shy."

I shut my mouth, and swallow the questions. *Why do you need protection? Why does he have to watch us?* I think of the money to distract me, picture crisp dollar bills so I won't have to think about the man, his eyes following our movement. He steps back, almost to the wall, and it helps slightly. He's already seen me give head; this isn't much different.

But sex *is* different. I may have gotten to the sad point where occasional hand and blowjobs occur, but sex has always been that *one* line I won't cross, proof to myself that I am not ruined, that I am still pure in some fucked-up form.

He leans forward and kisses me. The image of dollar bills disappears. Everything flees in the moment his lips touch mine.

A soft, sweet kiss. Not what I expect. He brushes my lips softly, and they part for him, wanting more. A groan slips from my mouth before I have a chance to capture it. His hands move up through my hair, gripping and pulling its strands. His tongue dips inside and I respond eagerly, my body taking over, shoving aside my thoughts as a wave of desire hits. His touch turns harder, his mouth more demanding and he moves me further into the suite, my heels skittering over wood floors, till the edge of the table bites into the back of my thighs.

His hands settle on my ass, squeezing it roughly, one hand on each cheek and lifts me easily, setting me on the table. The glass surface is cold, my bare pussy shocked by the sensation, my arousal throbbing to life. *Oh, hello there. Haven't seen you in a while.* The feeling is so foreign, so long-forgotten, that I almost smile.

"Lay back," he bites out against my lips, taking one last, torturous sweep of my mouth before stepping back, his hands yanking at his tie.

I grip the glass top, sliding backward until my elbows rest on the glass. I stay there, propped halfway up, and watch him unbutton one sleeve, then the second. His breath is hard, his eyes on mine and when he walks towards me, I can see the line of his arousal in his pants. He stops, still a few feet away.

He's an odd man. Cold to the point of being an asshole, and expecting me to perform as he demands. But I'm used to that. *Pleases* and *thank you's* aren't required, only appreciated. And despite his cold exterior, I am drawn to him, *insanely* attracted to him. Maybe it's the money, maybe it's as simple as that. But more likely it's that face, those blue eyes set under thick brows, a mess of dark hair that begs for hands to run through it, a strong jaw and kissable lips. Lips he happens to know exactly how to use.

My thoughts abandon me as he yanks his tie free and unbuttons his shirt, inch after inch of hard chest falling victim to my eyes. In his suit, he commanded respect. Without a shirt, he has my full attention, a perfect build unveiled as his shirt falls to the floor. I pull my eyes from his chest and return to his face, seeing the set of his jaw, the intensity of his eyes. I hear the yank of a zipper, and my eyes can't help but drop.

He is magnificent, every line and muscle defined, framing a package that makes my mouth and sex water. This is the organ that I have already experienced, one that kept me awake last night and started a fruitless self-pleasure session. I swallow as he steps closer, his eyes drifting over my naked body, his hand reaching out and pressing on my sternum, lying me flat before him on top of the table.

His hands touch my legs, lifting and tugging them outward, opening me wide before him. He bends, his hands on my ankle, his fingers unstrapping my heel, a loud thud sounding when the platform stiletto hits the floor. Then he moves to the other shoe, my foot lifting under his hand when it is free. He grabs an ankle in each hand and places my feet flat on the table, knees pointing to the ceiling.

"Touch yourself," he rasps, stepping back and watching me, his hand settling on and gripping his cock. It juts out, swollen and hard. The knowledge that I've caused that reaction is powerful, the vision of him stroking his cock the most carnal thing I've ever seen.

I close my eyes. I need the darkness, need to come down from sensory overload. I attempt to ignore my open legs, the view on display for the two men in the room. I touch myself tentatively, my finger sliding up and down my wet slit, slow gentle strokes that fan the already raging fire.

"Is that what you like?" I flinch at his voice, closer than I expected, and open my eyes, seeing him above me, looking down in between my legs, his hand moving up and down his delicious shaft.

I nod. "Initially, yes."

"Keep going."

I close my eyes again, my fingers never pausing in their travels, moisture collecting between my lips, my fingers grazing hot liquid as they move slowly and leisurely over the edge of my sanity. I allow one finger to dip in, to test my readiness, and drag some of that moisture higher, to the sensitive bud that is my pleasure center, circling the skin gently. I release a low moan, the building pleasure too great to contain, and arch my back, lifting slightly off the table as my fingers dance lightly through a torturous tease.

My pussy is beginning to respond, to flex and pant, saliva dripping from its eager lips. I can feel my clit taking attention, hardening beneath my gentle swipes, each circle moving a little closer. I am a sadistic bitch when it comes to masturbation, and my body loves me for it. I give until it wants and then I withdraw, coaxing my arousal out only to deny it. I won't come until it begs, until it screams for mercy, the explosion sweeter and more intense the longer I fuck with its mind.

I am reminded of my situation by a bite. Gentle scrapes of teeth against my nipple, first the left, and then the right. His mouth softens, sucking them into the heat of his mouth, his tongue dancing over the rough path of his teeth, my hand reaching up and grabbing his head, gripping that delicious mess of hair and bringing his head harder on my breasts, the sensation too incredible not to savor.

He yanks my hand off of his head, shoving it back between my legs, his message clear. I moan in frustration, stopping the sound when his mouth returns, visiting my other breast, the combination of soft mouth and hard teeth driving me wild.

"I'm close," I gasp, my sex contracting and screaming for release, my clit one swipe away from explosion. His mouth moves between my breasts, his fingers replacing his tongue, dragging them over my nipples, gentle and light enough to make them ache for more. His mouth, that incredible, hot machine of ecstasy, moves, traveling into the curves of my neck, and all I can think about is how it would feel between my legs.

"Come," he orders, his mouth lifting off my skin, one of his hands gripping my face and turning it to his, his blue eyes holding me hostage. "Come," he repeats, need blatant in his taunt, strong face.

I try to keep the eye contact, try to give him what I think he wants, but it is too strong – that final moment that my clit has been waiting for, that perfect swipe across its swollen surface has my eyes rolling back, my world temporarily going black, his blue eyes disappearing from sight as my back arches and I explode in

one.

perfect.

moment.

CHAPTER 7

I am weak, drained, my body losing all muscle function as the last tendrils of pleasure gently fade away, aftershocks twitching my body.

"Get up and get on the bed. I'm going to fuck the hell out of you." His voice is hoarse with need, the order almost a plea despite the command in his tone.

I roll to one side, my limbs sluggish, and sit up, eyeing the drop from the table to the floor. I am aided by his hands, helping me to my feet and then guiding me down a short hall and into the bedroom.

He spins me slowly, the dim lights of the bedroom blurring, and then I am facing him, his mouth finding mine, his hands gripping my waist and lifting me up and backward, onto the soft bed. I lay back and he crawls above me, the thick length of him stiff and heavy against my thighs. I part my legs and he settles between them, his mouth brushing across my throat, soft kisses alternating with delicate nips, his tongue teasing and torturing the hollows of my neck.

His hand reaches down, adjusting his cock, the hard shaft heavy and warm between my legs. He grinds forward, a hard thrust that creates a delicious friction between my legs. His lips pull off my neck, hovering above my mouth and he changes the pace, shortening his movement as he smoothly slides his bare cock over me. I inhale sharply, the ache between my legs growing, each withdrawal giving me hope that he will move it two inches lower and bury it inside of me.

I'm going to lose my mind. Between our bodies, I can almost feel the crackle of intense need. I can feel my heartbeat between my legs, the jitter of my muscles, everything itching for his touch. Everything about him screams domination, his touches hard and aggressive, each order sending a jolt of arousal through me. I've never yearned for submission before, never felt so eager to offer my body for his use.

He pulls off me, disappearing for a brief moment, then returns, his hands rolling over his cock, shielding it with a thin skin of latex. There is the soft shift of the mattress as he climbs onto the bed, positioning himself between my legs. His eyes meet mine. "Tell me what you want."

I don't respond. I can't think, can't even formulate a thought, not when his cock is bobbing before me, just inches from my wet cunt. He grips my legs, pulling me closer, and opening my legs and body to him. His stiff head bumps against my swollen lips, and I inhale sharply. It's the look in his eyes that is the most arousing. Possessive, dominating, with a fire behind them that both terrifies and electrifies me. There is a raw need in their depths, a demand in their intensity. He leans forward, grips the back of my neck and pulls me closer, his breath hot on my lips. "*Tell me*," he repeats.

I resist, my eyes glued to his, my body swooning when he reaches down, pressing his thick tip against my soaked opening. My eyes snap closed, the pending sensation too good not to savor. He shoves forward in one tiny motion, giving me just one thick inch, and I hiss through my teeth. *Holy hell.* Just that one inch, and my body reacts in a way I've never experienced, satisfying a carnal need I never knew I could have.

"TELL. ME." he grits, his mouth against mine, close enough to touch, but just enough space to torture. He pushes in another inch, then withdraws slowly. I moan in anguish.

"You," I whisper.

"Louder."

"You," I say stronger, almost crying out the word as his gaze burns into mine. "Your cock. Now. *Please.*" I lose all composure on the last word, my thighs trembling, voice breaking, and in the crack of the vowels, he fully thrusts, giving me all of him, my eyes snapping shut, head falling back. I claw at his shoulder, nails digging into muscle, needing to be close to him. He withdraws. Thrusts. Withdraws. My body memorizes his shape, contracts around his girth, and worships his stroke. Right now, during these minutes, he owns me. I am fully and completely his.

I wrap my legs, my heels digging into his perfect ass as he increases his pace, the slick sounds of our bodies mixing with hot breaths and rough kisses. He kisses like he will never get enough, feasting on my mouth while maintaining a fluid rhythm with his body, propping himself off of me with one hand while the other cradles my neck, holding me up to him.

I can't take much more of this, the furious pace building an animalistic need inside of me, a need that will only be fulfilled when I come. It's close, my core pulsing around his cock, our kiss interrupted by my gasp, and I whimper as my entire body tenses underneath his. "Don't stop," I beg, bucking backwards against his hand, my head rolling as the buildup reaches an overflow point, my orgasm on the edge of explosion. He releases me, bracing both hands on the bed and unleashes the full force of his cock, quick, fast thrusts that are perfect in rhythm, perfect in speed, and heavenly on my body. I risk a look upward, at the god above me, his body framed by city lights, his face determined and intense, the muscles of his chest and arms emphasized by the position, the overall package too much. The orgasm comes and it rips through me, tearing out sensibility and logic on its path, my body tensing underneath him, my heels gripping him tightly and my arms flail out, wrapping around his neck and pulling him closer, the movement doing nothing to slow the fuck, my orgasm stretched out with every pump of his muscular hips.

He doesn't give me time to rest, rolling over until I am on top, dizzy with lust, staring down on his beauty.

"Ride me." Dark, dangerous words, spoken with an edge.

I move, grinding my hips against him, a rolling motion.

"No. Up and down." He scowls and the expression does nothing but makes whatever vibe he rocks more devastating. I move my feet underneath me, resting my weight on them and move, lifting up and then down, feeling the immediate response of him inside me, his shaft thickening and straightening. I groan at the sensation, and settle fully down, the depth surprising me, the complete fullness something I've never experienced. He grips my waist and holds me down, thrusting slightly from below, my mouth opening slightly at the new sensation, my glazed eyes held by his, a cocky smile crossing his face.

That smile. It's deadly, yet I love its stab. He pins me against his chest and moves both of us upward, sliding along the bed until he is propped against the headboard and supported by pillows, sitting half up, the change affecting the angle, a delicious effect that has me shivering in pleasure.

"Fuck me." His words are strong, his eyes locked with mine, and his smile drops as need overtakes his features.

I move, sliding up and down in hard bounces, and he gives a tight nod of approval. I lift my hands to my breasts, the movement familiar, one from my typical lap dance routine. I squeeze them against my skin and am surprised by the change in his face. He sits up, and knocks my hands to the side, pinning my wrists behind my back. I pull, unable to free them and frown, his face now level with mine, inches away. I lean forward, trying for a kiss, wanting to calm whatever storm I have awakened, but he pulls back. "Keep riding," he rasps.

The new position is awkward, and I move to my knees, obediently continuing, my inner stretch indicating that my unknown foul has, in no way, affected his arousal. He grips my wrists harder, using them as resistance, and my fucks turn shallower as I move to the position he seems to want, my back arching, breasts offered up to him, his breath becoming ragged as I continue a hard rhythm up and down his cock.

"Perfect," he groans, holding my wrists tightly. "You are fucking perfect."

A compliment. I fight to hide my surprise, warmth spreading through my body at the words. They give me renewed confidence and I continue riding him, a gasp escaping me when his mouth lowers to my breasts. That thing he does, his alternation of teeth and tongue – it has a stronger effect than before, my entire body at a new, ungodly level of arousal, the buds of my breasts sensitive and crying out for the attention he lavishes with his mouth. I feel the press of his finger, gently on the pucker of my ass until it is given entrance, the tightness causing him to swear against my breasts, the added sensation causing me to tremble atop him.

"I can't—I'm about to..." My warning doesn't occur in time, my orgasm impatient, seizing my body in a full attack, my legs going still from the assault, pleasure ripping through me.

He takes over, panting against my chest as he fucks me from below, his finger deeper in my ass as I come apart, a cry ripping out of my throat, animalistic in its strength.

He's coming also, grunts coming from deep within his throat, his upward thrusts hard and fast. He releases my wrists and grips my waist, pulling me up and down in rhythm with his strokes. He roars, a primal bellow of ownership and his strokes slow as the sound fades, his mouth soft against mine as his hips slow, his arms wrapping tightly around my body and holding me solidly against him. His kiss marks me, strokes of his tongue speaking clearer than words, deepening the kiss as his cock softens inside of me. Then he pushes against my chest, rolling over and depositing me onto the bed, his bare body towering above me.

I stare up at him, my eyes making a slow and delicious journey over every curve, cut, and bulge of his body. The best sex of my life has officially wiped me out, every muscle a relaxed mess. He lets out a hard breath, then wipes his mouth and straightens.

CHAPTER 8

Silence. No purr of air conditioner, no television from another room. Dead silence as I lay on the bed and try to figure out what I am supposed to do. Follow him? Clean myself up? Roll over and go to sleep? Or is now when he returns with a handful of dollar bills? My lack of expertise in the prostitution gamble puts me at a loss.

Then, his silhouette returns, passing through the lit doorway. I prop myself up on one elbow and smile tentatively at him, wetting my lips to speak. My thoughts stall as he moves closer, his gait and build all wrong, too big for Nathan.

The man stops a foot from the bed, way too close for my personal comfort and I scramble for covers, for something to cover my nakedness.

"You should be used to men seeing you naked," he drawls, his voice a mix of husk and southern. He is close enough for me to see his features, to recognize his face. One of the bodyguards; the one who drove us here.

I pull the covers over my chest and glare at him. "I'm not at the strip club now."

It is a ridiculous statement, given that I am now at a point below that, having sex for money. But things are different outside the smoky glass doors of the club. Just because I undress at work doesn't give anyone and everyone a free look at my body. It is my body and right here, right now, I feel naked and want to cover up. Regardless of what this man has seen me do, I don't want him to see me like this.

He throws a white robe toward me. "The bathroom is yours if you

43

need it. We have a few things to go over, some calls to make. Feel free to make yourself at home."

"You always deliver his messages?" I scrunch my nose at him and he smiles.

"Most of the time."

It feels cold and transactional, and a feeling of unease sweeps through me. I thought we'd had a spark, a connection. I thought his kiss, the grip of his hand, the pant of his breath—I thought it all meant that he had ... I don't know what I thought. Yet, now, with the bodyguard glancing toward the door, I remember what this really is. One night. Maybe I should be grateful he isn't pushing me out the door.

Dance.
Suck it.
I'm going to fuck you.
Maybe communication isn't his forte.

I slip out of the bed, turning my back to the bodyguard, my mind whirring as I cinch the belt, the soft robe more luxurious than anything I have ever worn. I pull my hair out of the robe's neck, stalling as I try to sort through things in my head.

"If you need anything, we'll be on the balcony."

I nod. "Thank you."

He steps backward, out of the bedroom, and gently shuts the door.

NATHAN

"You need to be kinder to her." Drew speaks quietly, despite the closed balcony door, and the stiff ocean breeze.

"I don't want her to care for me."

Drew chuckles. "I don't think there's any fear of that. Right now, you need to be more concerned about her running from you."

"And go where? Back to that shithole house?" Nathan takes a long pull of bourbon. "She's smart enough to know better than that."

"I'm just saying, it wouldn't hurt to make her feel a little more comfortable. Especially if you want her to sign the papers."

Ah, yes. The papers. Just the thought of them filled him with a mix of anticipation and dread. In some ways, this plan was insane. In other ways, it was the only option.

He lifts the heavy tumbler to his mouth and buys a moment of time.

"Are we going to talk about tonight?" Drew's voice is as cold as he's ever heard it.

"Which part?"

"The part where you fucked her. I thought this plan was to do more of a wine and dine sort of thing."

The man has a point. But that plan had been concocted before he'd seen her body, before her lips had first wrapped around his cock. From that point on, it had only been a matter of when, and not if, he would fuck Candace Tapers.

He stands, glancing in the dark glass of the bedroom, the curve of her body barely visible under the spread.

"I'm gonna be married to the woman," he drawls. "It only makes sense that I know what I'm signing myself up for."

CHAPTER 9

Light streams through the open balcony doors, the smell of salt in the air, the sound of ocean waves soothing. I roll over, the sheets soft and smooth against my naked skin. I run a hand over the empty place where Nathan had slept. He had come to bed late, after I had taken a shower and lain in bed long enough to second-guess every minute of the evening. I had woken up when he had settled into the bed, the mattress moving slightly, the covers pulling across my hip. I hadn't moved, had only waited, hopeful that he would slide an arm across my body, or plant a kiss on the back of my neck.

He hadn't. He had lain as still as a corpse, his breaths shallow until the moment he had fallen asleep. I had wanted so badly, at that moment, to roll over and into his side, to rest my head on his chest and my arm across his body.

I haven't slept with a man since Seth. Most guys—the good guys—don't want to date a stripper. Fuck them, sure. Actually sleep with them? Cuddle and caress? *Nah.*

"Good morning."

I turn my head, my gaze colliding with a set of green eyes, ones that lead to a crooked nose, full lips and a few days of unshaven growth. *The security guy. Some name that begins with a D. Drew.*

"Mr. Dumont would like to speak to you."

I stretch, a long and lazy motion that fully utilizes every inch of the king bed, then sit up, holding the blanket against my chest. "Do you mind getting my dress from out there?"

"There is a set of clothes for you in the closet. You may be more comfortable in those."

I turn my head and eye the closet door. "Okay."

When he leaves the room, I throw off the blanket and stand up.

The closet is empty, except for a few padded hangers. One holds a flannel set of pajamas, ones I would have appreciated last night. I roll my eyes and flip to the next hanger, which has a pale blue sundress and matching cardigan. I pull it loose, the tags snagging on the hanger, and I pause, carefully separating the items. My eyes catch on the price tag, and I let out a low whistle. Three hundred dollars for a sundress? A bit excessive for a sending-the-hooker-on-her-way outfit.

I pull the dress carefully over my head, leaving the tags on. I don't work on Tuesday. Maybe I can return it then, assuming he bought it somewhere locally. I think again of the Nashville address on his license, and my stomach flips, a reminder of the fact that my life is about to return to normal.

"Candy?" There is the soft knock on the bedroom door, and I run a quick hand through my hair.

"Coming." My eyes drop to the floor, where a pair of lace panties lie next to some wedge sandals. I crouch down, pulling the tags off the panties and snagging the wedges. Brian Atwoods, in my size, a fact that gives me a serious moment of pause.

Is this creepy? A pre-purchased outfit in my size? Maybe it's sweet. Maybe he planned ahead and … I end that thought process. There is no "planning ahead" scenario that isn't creepy.

I pull on the panties and straighten the lay of the dress, carrying the shoes and pulling open the bedroom door. The bodyguard steps away from the door, gesturing me forward.

"He's at the table."

I smile breezily at him, my excitement mounting at the thought of getting paid. I wonder if he'll give me a fat stack of bills, something thick and impressive. Or maybe a check, though he doesn't seem like that type.

I round the corner and slow, spying Nathan at the table, a spread of documents before him. He slides the chair backward and stands at my approach.

"Good morning, Candace. Please, sit down."

CHAPTER 10

I look at the document in confusion, the pages filled with words that don't belong near me.

Marriage.
Prenuptial.
Assumption.
Loyalty.
Confidentiality.

I set down the pages and look at him, sitting on the other end of the long dining table. The same table on which I had laid naked, touched myself on, begged him from.

"I'm confused…" I glance back down, my name in the first sentence, in clear block font. "Is this document for me?"

"It's a proposal. Last night was an audition of sorts. To see if we are sexually compatible. I have strong sexual needs, and you prove equipped to handle them. I need, for various reasons, a wife. I've had you followed for several weeks. You seem to have a fairly despondent life, with no boyfriend, no family, no financial security. I am offering you a business proposition."

So many bombs to deliver. *I've had you followed for weeks.* The statement fills me with a mix of anger and fear, my ignorance of the situation alarming. I think of Dib's house, the overgrown yard, my dented car with duct tape over one fender, and flush from embarrassment. *No family.* That's incorrect, an observation that is either truly ignorant, or disdainfully hateful. I have a father. Whether I visit enough, or lie to him about my life, or can't afford to move him to a nicer facility—all of that is immaterial to the fact that he exists. I swallow. "I have family. My father. He's in a hospital in Jacksonville."

He says nothing, and if I expected sympathy, I was wrong.

I glance back down at the documents, my mind clogged with possibilities, in equal amounts fear and excitement. "I don't see a compensation structure."

That produces a laugh, one short bark absolutely devoid of humor. "Compensation?"

I meet his mocking eyes. "Yes. Business propositions involve compensation on both parts. I understand what I am giving up, but fail to see what I am getting from this arrangement."

He holds out his hands, gesturing to the suite. "This *life*. You are barely struggling by. I am offering you a life of luxury, with everything you want, at your fingertips. You won't have to work, will no longer have to straddle sweaty men with wandering hands."

I arch a brow. "Oh. Like you?"

He pushes back from the table and stands. "Look at the paperwork. If you are interested, sign the documents. If not, Drew will give you your money and take you home. Either way, you will be paid." He turns, grabbing a jacket off the counter and shrugging into it.

I stand and the chair scrapes the floor, the raw sound loud in the quiet suite. "Is this your idea of romance?"

He stops on his way past me, turning slightly, his eyes lighting with amusement. "Romance?"

Just steps away, the close proximity gives me the full force of his eyes, the morning light turning them turquoise in color and I am surprised to see a hint of playfulness in their depths. "Yes, romance. Isn't that what *marriage* is all about? Isn't that what these papers are about? Me agreeing to be your wife?"

He chuckles, and I'm glad this entire thing is so entertaining to him. "I need a *wife*. I am not signing up for romance, or affection, or a full time job. The papers will discuss your duties. I want nothing more from you than what is stated there. And as far as you – you should *never* expect that from me." His voice changes, the amusement gone, and the next words out of his mouth, I fully believe. "I will not love you. I will have no use for you other than sex and photo ops. That is something you might want to consider when making your decision."

It is the most he has ever said, and what I understand from it far surpasses the short speech. I step back, tripping over the chair before catching myself. He doesn't move, doesn't reach out, doesn't offer a hand. He only watches me, our eyes meeting for a long battle of silent communication, one I don't win.

Then he turns, and leaves, the door slamming against the frame.

***

I sit, my eyes drawn to the papers. I am now alone with Drew, a man whose presence is distracting, the weight of his stare heavy on my back. I read the first paragraph three times, the words blurring, my brain unable to focus. I turn my head slightly. "Do you mind leaving me alone? I'm trying to think, which is hard with you breathing down my neck."

"There's not really anything to think about." His voice echoes in the small space, and I lift my head from my reading.

"What's *that* supposed to mean?"

"I've seen your life. That creature you live with, that dirty club you work at. He picked you because you are better than that. Because you have the qualities he wants. Most women with your qualities are in a lifestyle that they are comfortable with. They aren't going to leave their lives behind, no matter how big his bank account is. You are a unique breed in a unique situation."

"And you are sharing this information with me because…" I set down the papers and lean back, looking into those green eyes, trying to sort the bullshit from the truth. The problem is, everything he is saying is just wretched enough to be true.

"Because I know what you are thinking. I know that you are about to take the ten thousand dollars and ask me to take you home. And you will have a temporary reprieve from your misery. But then life will return and you will be in the same position as before. You cannot rise above your current life if you are always one paycheck away from homelessness."

One paycheck away from homelessness. A sobering thought. Was it true?

Jez would take me in for a week or two, offering up her couch and a worn sheet. But she struggles as I do, all of us selling our bodies at an exchange rate that is far too low. My college friends have all moved on, my shame causing me to cut all ties when I began to strip. As for family... my mother passed on four years ago, ovarian cancer taking her quickly. My father... he needs *my* help right now, not the other way around.

The doctors can't figure out what's wrong with him. Six months ago he fell sick, and now his health insurance is close to maxing out, our last conversation one of heavy stress. Ten thousand dollars would be swallowed by his bills. I haven't seen him in almost two years. He thinks I'm a wedding planner, that my busy schedule won't allow a visit. The reality is that I haven't had the money to take time off and stay with him in the hospital. Plus, there is the five hour drive in my car. With the dry cough of my engine, the shimmy that occurs over forty miles per hour, and the worn tread of my tires, the probability of being stranded on the side of the highway is too high.

It's depressing to take such a critical life inventory. I've never allowed myself to dwell on it before because, really, I've had no options. I've focused on one day at a time, and the years have passed, the time marked by late rent payments and the appearance of wrinkles – tiny ones, on the corners of my eyes. They are a reminder of the hourglass that we all live in, grains of sand slipping through the gap of time, each granule adding another wrinkle, another pocket of fat, another sag that I will have to fight to overcome, another grey hair to pluck or dye. My earning potential is at the highest point of the arc right now, and that is a terrifying reality.

But we all know that our best chances lay in the clients. And here is my client, offering—not romance, but a contract, a *business* proposition. A proposition that I should strongly consider.

The man speaks, interrupting my thoughts. "There is another piece of the process. If you decide to stay here, the contract is contingent on acceptable test results." If I didn't know better, I'd say there was almost in an apology in the words.

"What kind of tests?" I laugh. "Is there an intelligence requirement?"

"We already have your college records and test scores. I'm referring to blood tests."

My face flushes at the thought of my college transcript. My grades had been average at best, indicative of my lack of interest in anything but keg stands and happy hours. "What's the reason for the blood tests?"

"A combination of things. A full STD workup, pregnancy test, genetic markers, drugs. Do you foresee a problem with any of those things?"

I shake my head, though I'm not certain of what they might yield. I've been practically celibate since Scott, the strip club not a conducive environment for meeting quality men. But they say you can get STDs from oral sex, a fairly important piece of information I have conveniently ignored.

"Great." He steps away from the table. I'll let Mr. Dumont know."

I clear my throat. "Please let Mr. Dumont know that I will require my own set of tests. Anything I am being tested for, I would like him also tested for. *I* may not be happy with the results of *his* tests." I huff out the words, frustrated with the tests, the legalese of the contract, and being sideswiped with this life-changing decision. I let out a low growl and pick up the document, attempting to work through the fourth paragraph.

"Very well, Ms. Tapers. I'll let Mr. Dumont know your demands. I don't imagine he will have an issue with that."

There is the blessed sound of his exit and I am alone at the table, trying to make sense of eight pages of legal confusion. *Ms. Tapers.* Proof that they *have* done their homework, proof that I have been watched, followed, researched. And all I have about my prospective husband is a name. Nathan Dumont.

I reach out, my fingers struggling to snag the handle of my purse without standing up. When I finally get it, I pull out my phone to Google him, but the battery is dead.

Good thing these people don't seem crazy. Next time I decide to be kidnapped by a group of strangers, I'll pack a charger. I set down the phone and turn back to the document.

CHAPTER 11

The contract loses me more than it guides me, covered in *wherefores* and *hereafters*. When I don't understand something, I forge on, hoping that the next sentence will give me a clearer understanding. When I reach the second page, I pick my purse back up, shifting through it until I find a pen. I return to the first page, underlining, circling, and scribbling words into the margins. I'm not exactly sure what the hell I am doing. It's a waste of time reading this. I could be in the limo, ten grand richer, headed back home.

I turn the page.

> The female in question, hereafter referred to as "Wife", will be restricted from contact with any past relationships, regardless of gender and familial relation, with the exception of Wife's Father, Harold Tapers. Wife will be allowed weekly visits with Harold Tapers, and will have use of Husband's private plane and pilot to conduct these visits.

I frown. Nathan had acted as if I had no family, yet here is my father's name. Harold Tapers. Weekly visits. Private plane. I underline the words, the line a little wobbly in its execution.

> Husband agrees to pay for any and all medical bills pertaining to Mr. Tapers, hereafter referred to as "Father", for the duration of the Marriage, in addition to accepting financial obligation for said Father's living expenses.

Somewhere inside my chest, there is a release of stress, a cracking of bones, something that opens my lungs wider and allows my first full breath in years. I blink, my eyes damp, and let out a shaky breath.

> Wife will not be given any cash, but will be assigned two (2) credit cards for her personal shopping and travel needs. She will be allowed the purchase of one new car every two years, but current car must be traded in on the new vehicle purchase.

I continue reading, thinking about my father's medical tests that insurance denied, the medication copays, the—I force myself to stop, to take another breath, to read on.

> Wife is entering into this agreement in the possession of Ten Thousand Dollars ($10,000.00). Such property is listed in **Marital Prenuptial Agreement** and will be and remains the property of the Wife and the Husband will have no right to or interest in such present property.

> Wife will be allowed to have hobbies, given that those hobbies do not take her away from the Marital Home at times inconvenient to Husband. Wife will be allowed to have friends, but they must be pre-approved by Husband, social standing being of primary importance in the Marriage. If friendships become unpleasing to Husband, they will be terminated by Wife.

It sounds like I'm entering into a 1950's marriage. I put a frowny face next to the words *pre-approved* and *unpleasing*. Not that it really matters. I haven't had real friends in a really long time. I won't be pulling at the bit for new ones.

> Wife agrees to terminate all ties with previous occupation, residence, and lifestyle. She will consent to a Legal Name Change (Candace Dumont) and will keep all details of her prior lifestyle confidential.

I turn to the next page, where the contract turns to our marital sexual lifestyle, desexualized by staunch and clinical terms.

> Wife will submit to Husband in all matters sexual. She will not have the right to dictate sexual positions, fornication locations, or duration thereof. Husband agrees that his Sexual Expectations will be limited to one (1) Sexual Penetration Act per day, with the understanding that Wife can initiate additional Sexual Acts if she chooses. Husband is not required to perform Sexual Acts with Wife.

I shift in the chair, both freaked-out and aroused by the words. I'm not surprised that he'd want control of our sex life. Dominance seems to be his thing. I take a small sip of the ice water that sits at my place, and fight the urge to fan myself.

> Wife will maintain a strict regimen of Birth Control Pills. If and when Husband and Wife decide to have children, an Amendment to this Marriage Agreement will be agreed upon. Wife agrees that, in the event of an Unplanned Pregnancy, she will not terminate the pregnancy unless she has written approval from Husband.

Children? How long does he expect our fake marriage to last? I set down the contract. It appears to be a carefully controlled fairytale. All of the luxuries of a dream lifestyle, hold the freedom and romance. I am almost grateful for the bulleted points, the discussion of every aspect of my future life as Wife. It is all here, in these eight pages. The instruction manual for the next chapter in my life. And, as unromantic as this arrangement is, as segmented and dictating as Nathan appears to be, he is also—through these eight pages— transparent. A known evil, when the last couple of years have been a landmine of unknown ones.

I flip to the final page, the last line very simple and very permanent.

> The Marriage will be executed within thirty (30) days of this agreement.

Below that, a signature block, his name already scrawled in thick blue ink above his name. I move down to my own, rolling the pen softly in my fingers as I stare at the solid line that could change my life forever.

PART TWO

Life as a trophy wife? Piece of freaking cake.

NATHAN

He unlocks the suite and steps inside, his eyes meeting Drew's, who gives a stiff nod and takes the pen from the blonde who will become his new wife. Striding forward, Nathan holds out a hand for the pages.

She's watching him. He can feel her gaze, as he checks her signature and re-caps the pen. He glances up, and she holds his stare for a moment, then glances away.

"So…" she sits back in the chair, adjusting the bodice of the sundress. "I guess you and I are getting married."

"It would appear so." He tucks the pen in his jacket, and drops a plastic bag on the table, pushing it toward her. "Your new phone."

She perks up, leaning forward and opening the bag, her expression changing when she sees the simple flip phone. "Wow," she muses, with all of the enthusiasm of an aloof cat. "You shouldn't have."

"As my wife, you won't be on social media, or communicating with anyone from your old life." He nods to Drew, who pulls her purse off of the floor and rummages through it, tossing a cracked iPhone, the case covered in fake diamonds, toward him. He glances at it, then sets it down on the table.

"Hey!" she half stands, pushing back from the table, and his eyes drop to her outfit, the expensive fabric hanging well off her curves. After they reach Nashville, and the Fenton team begins, she'll look even better. Fake marriage or not, he damn well isn't going to have a rough looking wife. "Give me that!" she gestures to the iPhone.

He doesn't move. "Think of this as a job, Candace. I am your new employer. You can't have a phone at work. You can't have a past at work. If you want to quit and walk out that door tomorrow—fine. But while you are married to me, you *will* follow my rules."

"Your rules seem ridiculous," she snaps back. "You're not going to chain me to a basement wall somewhere, are you?" Her forehead pinches, and a flash of alarm shows, as she considers this new possibility.

"I can assure you, there will be no basements or imprisonment involved. Though if you'd like to be tied up, that is certainly something I can arrange." He presses his lips together in an attempt to halt the grin.

She likes that. She pretends she doesn't, her glare intensifying, a snort of irritation coming out, but she fucking likes it. Right now, if he walks forward and pushes her back in that chair, his fingers sliding up her bare thigh, to the crotch of those silk panties, she'll be wet. Just the thought of it, of her stretched across his bed, her skin pink, her ankles spread … it is getting him hard. And that is going to be a serious problem, his reactions to her. He is supposed to be marrying her for a purpose, something he's forgetting every time their eyes meet.

"We should head out." Drew pockets her phone. "There's a storm coming we should get in front of."

"Where are we going?" She pushes to her feet, and there is almost a childlike quality to her movements, a hesitant excitement at the adventure ahead.

"Nashville," he supplies. "My—our house there. And don't worry, it doesn't have a basement."

She rolls her eyes at the response, slipping the cheap purse over her shoulder and stepping past him. Drew follows, a warning in his gaze. A warning Nathan chooses to ignore.

CHAPTER 12

There's no basement, no chains, just a line of private planes, Nathan's second lackey—Mark—helping me inside. The trip doesn't take long, and Nathan doesn't pull out his dick, the entire ride completed without any interaction at all. It appears I am marrying a non-talker.

Marrying. I swallow, and look out the window, unsure whether to pinch or slap myself. Is this actually happening? The decision leaves an odd taste in my mouth, my tongue unsure whether to celebrate the flavor or spit it out.

The limo slows, coming to a stop before a large neighborhood gate. Nathan glances up from his phone, listening to the conversation between his security man—Drew—and the guard. "Drew's giving them your information." He glances at me, and it's the first eye contact we've had in hours. "They'll quickly learn your face."

My chances of death and dismemberment diminish slightly. I let out a breath, then think of something. "My car—it's still at Sammy's." I picture my sad Subaru, bird droppings collecting on its blue paint, pollen coating its surface, drunk patrons writing crude remarks in the dusty windows.

"We are having it, and all of your belongings, moved to a storage unit." He looks down at his phone, as if that snippet of information doesn't dump out my innards and stomp right through them.

"*Who* is doing all that?" I turn in my seat, facing him, my question ignored. I reach out a hand, covering his phone's screen. He sighs, his jaw tightening, and when he glances up, the irritation in his eyes almost causes me to back off. Almost. "I have personal items in there. I don't want one of your guys going through all of my stuff."

"Fine," he snaps, and holds out his phone. "Call one of your friends. Tell them they have a week to pack up your shit. I'll have movers pick up any boxes from your old house then." He waits, his phone outstretched, and it looks a hell of a lot nicer than my new one.

I glance down at it, then turn, leaning on the armrest and looking out the window. "Never mind." I blow out a breath. "Just have your guys do it." My pride can't tell him the truth. I don't think I have a friend who'd want to bother with it.

We slow down again, a monstrous mansion to our right, and stop before another set of gates. A bit overkill. The gates open and I lean forward, curious.

The limo pulls around the drive, thick bushes passing, the home unveiled as we roll forward. It's a voyeur's dream, glass the primary building material, and I look through the house and at the view, rolling hills and the glitter of a lake visible. "Your Windex budget must be out of control."

"I wouldn't know." He reaches out, placing a hand on my bare knee, halting my reach for the door handle. "I'll have Drew show you around. He can answer any questions you may have."

"You're not coming in?" I watch as he releases my knee, his eyes already back on his phone. My door is opened, and I hold up a hand to block the glare.

"I'm heading to the office." He nods in the general direction of the house, and it's as strong as a push. I accept Drew's hand and step from the car, distracted by the thought of Nathan as I inhale everything about this new world.

Honeysuckle, the scent faint on the air, the bright green lawn punctuated by blocks of flowerbeds, all spilling with colors and textures, the soft sound of a sprinkler humming in the background. The home is white and modern, the glass walls showcasing low-slung furniture and bold art. A few years ago, I'd flipped through an Architectural Digest and torn out pages of a home like this. A few years ago, I'd have given anything for it. Now, I would have been happy with hot water and a genie to remove all of my debt.

Nathan wasn't removing my debt, but he was doing one step better—taking care of my father. On the drive to the Destin airport, he'd presented me with two brochures, one for a facility an hour outside of Nashville—one for a facility in Jacksonville, close to Dad's current home. I pocketed both, deciding to let my father decide, but not before I saw their rates, the figures causing my stomach to knot. For Nathan, it may be nothing. For me, and for my father, it is everything.

"Coming?" Drew stands at the front doors.

I force a smile, and step forward.

***

The tour doesn't take long, the common areas quickly addressed. Media room. Gym. Great room. Dining room. Kitchen. We swing by Nathan's office, and skip one hallway altogether.

"What's down there?" I slow, and Drew all but pushes me forward.

"My room, and the laundry. You won't have need of either."

"You *live* here?" I stop, visions of newly-wed romantic time clashing with the idea of bumping into Drew in the middle of the night.

"Will that be a problem, princess?" He crosses his arms over his chest, and I can see why Nathan would hire him, his intimidation factor high, his build impressive. In my wedges, I still only come to his shoulder.

I shrug. "It just seems weird."

We cross through the great room, and to the other end of the house. Drew opens a door, and we step into the master suite.

Dark tile floors. Rich blue walls. A huge bed that sits atop a fur rug. The fireplace from the great room also opens into this, and I envision myself, naked on the rug, the fire's warmth on our bodies, Nathan above me. I swallow a smile.

"His bathroom is through there." He gestures to an arched opening, and I can see a jetted tub and the edge of a shower. I turn back, and watch him move to the windows, pulling at a handle, the entire wall sliding into itself and opening to the backyard. "Your room is out here."

My room? I hurry forward, stepping over the transom and almost trip down a set of steps, following him along the side of a pool and toward a guesthouse. I stop. The guesthouse is a miniature version of the main home, right down to the identical fireplace and all glass walls. It's a fish bowl, and I can see its entire layout without setting foot inside. A bedroom, with a seating area and desk. A bathroom. Mini-kitchenette. Fireplace. *My room.*

He opens the sliding door and turns to me.

"I'm confused…" I glance back at the main house, that contained at least two guest rooms, if my tour's memory serves correct. "I'm not staying with Nathan?"

"No." He steps in, holding the door open for me.

"Why not?"

"Why would you?"

This is exasperating. "Because I'm his *wife?*"

"In name only. You're forgetting that this is a business arrangement, not a romance."

"A business arrangement where he fucks me?" It feels crude, saying the words in this environment of expense and class.

He sighs. "Nathan isn't great at being told he can't have something. I'd apologize for his actions, but you seem to enjoy them."

I snap my mouth shut, no good comeback springing to mind.

Drew glances at his watch. "I'll let you get acquainted here. The others will be arriving in a half hour, if you want to freshen up.

I raise a brow at him. "The others?"

***

The others. They invade like a hoard of zombies, knocking over planters and clawing past curtains in their haste to pull at my hair, scrape razors over my skin and wield tweezers with sadistic zest.

Okay, maybe it isn't that bad. I lift up the edge of the gel mask and glance down at my feet and the woman perched before them. "What color are you painting them?" When I ask the question, half of my face mask cracks.

"Nude," Rosit Fenton barks, scurrying over in a swish of Burberry plaid and cream. "From now on, Candace, only nude on your nails. It's a rule."

Another rule. I roll my eyes. I should start writing them down. Drew had, after depositing me into this glass prison, rattled off a few of them. No entering the house after dark. No roaming the house unescorted. No having fun, though that question wasn't so much stated as implied. "Nude nails. Got it."

"While I have you…" Rosit drawls. "Let's discuss the other problem areas." There is the squeak of wheels against tile and I watch him wheel my desk chair forward, his chubby legs scooting along the floor in the way that a dog would drag his ass across carpet.

"*More* problem areas?" I groan. I had no idea I was such a beauty train wreck. Between the facial, and the teeth whitening, and fake nails removal, I am feeling a little insecure.

"Honey, we haven't even gotten started." He peers at a clipboard, then looks critically at my face. "We've still got waxing, lash extensions, cellulite reductions and your diet and exercise regimen to discuss."

I groan. "Please, just go away."

"Oh yes," he intones. "It's so hard to be well taken care of. We all feel absolutely terrible for you." He pats my arm in the most condescending manner possible, and a sliver of guilt hits. Maybe I *am* acting a little spoiled. It isn't like any of this is painful. And once I get this gunk off my face, and this tent off my hair, I'll probably love the final product. I force a smile, and firmly instruct myself to relax and enjoy myself. I close my eyes and sink into the recliner, letting all of my stress and fears go.

I can do this. Life as a trophy wife? Piece of freaking cake.

***

I wheeze out a breath, the pain jolting through me. It's the anticipation of it that is the worst, not knowing when or where it will come, no warning given, each second of waiting agonizingly long.

There is another red bite of pain, and I buck off of the table, screaming out a curse.

"Be still!" The woman snaps at me, her nails digging into my stomach as she presses me down. "Next time, don't shave first. It makes it hurt more."

There's not going to be a next time. As soon as I can walk, as soon as I can *stand*, I am going to hobble my way into Nathan's house and tell him that he can stick a wax stick up his ass—I'm never doing this again. The woman yanks again, ripping out the tiny hairs that line my perineum, and I choke back a sob.

***

I stare at a stranger. When I lean forward, so does she. I run a hand through my hair—thick dark strands—and watch the way it shimmers in the bathroom's light.

It's a miracle.

Not that I wasn't a pretty girl before. I've always been pretty, in that hot rod magazine way, a look I enhanced with bleached blonde hair and fake nails, glitter mascara and tan skin adding an extra bit of oomph to my appeal.

Now, I'm all woman. I frown, my wrinkles gone, courtesy of Botox injections. I smile and past my plump, freshly exfoliated lips, brilliant white teeth glisten. My blue eyes—enhanced with color contacts—glow, surrounded by a thick frame of false eyelashes, trimmed to an appropriate natural length.

I cross my legs, and marvel at the smooth feel of the waxed skin. Maybe I will do it again. Just once or twice.

I look down at the booklet before me, turning a page over, and scanning the two outfits featured on the page. Next to each outfit's items are numbers, which match hangers in my new closet. It is a mix and match system designed for the most idiotic of users. I am supposed to pick an outfit from the book, select the corresponding hangers from the closet, and dress. The book is a waste of time, since everything in the closet is either white, black or cream. I'll have to work pretty hard to fuck up that color combination.

There is the rap of knuckles against the glass, and I turn, seeing Mark slide open the door. "There's food in the fridge if you'd like some."

I glance at the clock, realizing that it is almost seven. "What's Nathan doing for dinner?"

"He's already eaten." The disappointment must have shown on my face. "You won't be having your meals together, not unless he needs you for some reason. I'll be sure to let you know in advance, if I can."

There's no reason for me to be irritated by the news. As it has so clearly been explained to me, this isn't a romance. We aren't dating, or courting, or anything in that vein. *Think of this as a job, Candace. I am your new employer.* I push to my feet and smile at the man. "I'm actually starving. Could you show me the food?"

Fifteen minutes later, I stab a piece of broccoli and quietly lift it to my mouth, my eyes on the television screen. I chew the vegetable and glance toward the main house, the curtains all drawn, the light in Nathan's bedroom on. Tomorrow, I will get back on his plane and fly to Jacksonville to see my father. I cut a piece of grilled chicken. The fridge didn't just hold tonight's dinner. There were five prepackaged meals in the neatly labeled CANDACE stack, each with reheating instructions clearly printed on the lid. I chose the juiciest of the stack, a portion-controlled sampling that delivered the precise ration of carbs/protein/fat that had been preached to me in my afternoon nutritional session by a perky blonde named Beth.

I can already predict, with absolute certainty, that I will hate Beth. Our first physical training session is set for the day after tomorrow.

The lights dim in Nathan's room and I set aside the tray, eyeing the bank of curtains, pulled taut across his windows. I have my own set of curtains, I could close them and hide everything I am doing, the entire exciting process of eating dinner in my brand new silk pajamas. I intentionally left them open, thinking he might see me, might stop by. I had wanted to show him my new look, an adolescent need for approval rearing its ugly head. *Husband agrees that Sexual Expectations will be limited to one (1) Sexual Penetration Act per day.* That contract had been prepared before we had slept together in Rosemary Beach. Maybe he hadn't enjoyed it. Maybe we'd never have sex again. He certainly hadn't shown any interest since then. *Wife can initiate additional Sexual Acts if she chooses.* I push the tray to the side and settle back in the bed's pillows, pulling the covers up and reaching for the remote. There is no way I'm going to initiate anything with him. I close my eyes, and try to push the image of his face, the feel of his hand, out of my mind.

CHAPTER 13

I've got to get Dad out of here. I finger the ends of my hair, and lean, as subtly as possible, away from the man that sits beside me. He's a cougher, the sort of stranger that doesn't bother to cover his mouth, or—from the pungent smell drifting over—bathe. I should have sat on the other side, by the pregnant woman with the snot-covered kid. Poor planning. I sigh, tugging at a piece of hair before letting it go. My head feels strange, my waist-length tresses now glossy and thick, extensions added, my hair dyed the color of dark chocolate. My hair hasn't been brown since I was thirteen and discovered Sun-In.

My name is called, and I stand, swinging my bag, a Chanel that perfectly matches my linen slacks, over one shoulder. I move through a swinging door and follow the woman down a hall and presumably, toward my father. I glance in the open rooms that we pass, some crowded with guests, most empty, the feet of patients tenting the bottom of white sheets.

I want him out of here. I have the two brochures from Nathan in my purse. All I need to do is to tell my father to pick one. All I need to do is walk in and say hello.

It should be easy, yet my hand trembles as I tuck a piece of hair behind my ear. I should be excited, yet the guilt is all but suffocating me. I could have come. I could have gotten on a Greyhound, or rented a car, or found *some* way, in the six months since he fell sick, to come. There's no excuse that I didn't.

As we move closer, I second-guess my steps. Maybe I should have called ahead and warned him of my arrival. Maybe this sort of thing doesn't go well as a surprise.

The nurse stops in front of a room, and reaches forward, turning the handle. "You coming?" She peers at me in the irritated manner of an overworked woman.

I nod, and walk, smiling brightly, one designer heel stepping in front of another, past an intubated woman and the curtain that hides my father. The sole of my heel sticks to a rough place on the floor and I freeze at my first glimpse of him.

How can a man change so completely in two years? The paleness of his skin, the hollows that frame his eyes. He's lost twenty or thirty pounds, and I can see it in his face, in the thin neck that now flexes in his swallow of meds.

He sets down the plastic cup, moving the tray carefully aside, and glances up briefly, then stares. Puzzlement hits first, and then a crumble of composure, his body straining as he reaches out to me with trembling hands. I hurry forward, his hands fumbling over my shoulders, gripping me tightly, his watery eyes locking on mine. "Candace," he whispers. "Oh, Candace."

He holds me with a fierceness that alarms me, his need so great, a man who has been neglected too long. A sob catches me off guard, ugly in its wail, and it takes a moment for me to realize that it comes from me. I am suddenly wracked with too many emotions, guilt dominant, squashing all of the rest in its fight to the front.

My father, who had been so strong on our phone calls—so light-hearted and nonchalant.
"Sweetie, I'm fine."
"Don't worry about me, I'll fight this."
"The ladies at the hospital have been spoiling me rotten."

No one in this hospital is spoiling him. I'd be shocked if any of them even know his name.

His fingers tighten, gripping me as if I am his lifeline. Maybe I am. I am his only child, a child who had abandoned him in his time of need. I've been four short hours away, lying to my father, inventing a life that didn't exist so that I could excuse my lack of visitation. Ashamed of my job, ashamed of my life, my selfishness had left him to fight a lonely battle.

In this horrible moment, when I realize all the ways I've failed him, I know I've made the right decision. I will sign my soul to the devil if it means that I can, in some way, right my shortcomings as a daughter. He is my father, and, right here in his hospital room, I vow to become more worthy of his love.

NATHAN

The last woman he gave his heart to still has it. Sometimes he wonders if she ever looks at it, tends to it, nurtures it. Knowing Cecile, she probably just jabs it every once in a while, strictly for the hell of it.

Today, he felt her jab. He stood there, staring at a beautiful woman, and felt the painful poke of her memory. When Candace smiled, he saw Cecile's grin. When she ran a hand through her hair, he saw blond locks instead of brunette.

Maybe that's why he did what he did. Maybe that's why he pulled Candy from her spot at the kitchen sink, and bent her over the island. Maybe, had Cecile not been so present, he would have been gentler. Maybe he wouldn't have drilled into Candy without pause, pulled her against him without apology, fucked her without care.

Not that either of them seemed to mind. She came twice, her shrieks so loud they brought Drew out from his room, his eyes darkening at the sight, his retreat as quick as his entrance. And the orgasm... he stretches out his legs, his cock thickening at just the thought of it. His orgasm had wiped any thoughts of Cecile right out of his head. His orgasm had blinded his self-control, had destroyed his sanity, and left him kissing her mouth, her neck, her breasts. His orgasm had rendered him a passionate fool.

That's the beauty of sex. It can fuck up your world and then repair it all. Destroy your heart and then build you a new one. Turn you from heartbroken to love-struck in a hundred delicious thrusts.

Not that this was love. It couldn't be, and it wouldn't be. Not when Cecile still owned his heart.

CHAPTER 14

Dad's condition hasn't improved, but his setting certainly has. He's now an hour outside of Nashville, in a manicured resort called Crestridge. His private, corner room has windows that open to a bloom-filled garden. I grip his hand, grateful to feel a response, a tightening of his fingers around mine. "Hey beautiful," he whispers.

My eyes flit from his weak face to the monitor beside him. "Hey Daddy. How's your day going?"

"You know me. Just fighting off the ladies." He smiles at me, the motion breaking my heart in its lighthearted attempt.

"So I've heard. Janice at the front desk is positively glowing about you. Try to let her down easily."

He laughs, a loose sound that turns into a cough, his grip tightening as his body tenses. I hold my frown at bay, patting his hand gently. "I'm working on a new crossword puzzle. I'm stuck on a few. Think you could help me out?"

He nods, releasing my hand and gesturing for me to continue. I grin, reaching into my bag and pulling out a worn book, the second we are working through. Our first book was one for beginners, the clues ridiculously easy. This one is for intermediate puzzlers, and we are moving through it at a much slower pace. I can't pick up the book without fearing that we will never finish it. It, like everything else in my visits, is a bittersweet reminder of the time I have wasted, and how little we have left.

I settle back in the chair, my lower back flaring in pain. My body is revolting, displeased with my new workout regime. According to the

79

energetic ball of annoyance named Beth, I will be having my ass kicked for two hours a day, twice a week. Following that schedule, and my new diet, I will be down a dress size within thirty days. I reach back in my bag and pull out the Twix bar I snagged from the vending machine. I'm not particularly interested in losing a dress size. Not when every color coordinated outfit Rosit Fenton supplied me with is conservative as hell. I'm going to be killing myself for a body that no one will see. Well, no one besides Nathan.

I think of last night, how he had tossed a glass of wine into the sink and grabbed me, right as I was pulling my plate from the microwave. Any of my concerns over his attraction to me had ended in the twenty minutes of raw, animal fucking that he had given me.

I move my pen down to the last completed clue, double-checking my work before moving on to the next. I had been so pathetically grateful for the sex, the experience one of the only times Nathan had spoken or interacted with me all week.

I keep my voice low, giving Dad the clue and waiting as he thinks. He gets the answer quickly and I move on. After a half hour or so, his pauses lengthen, and during one long break, I open the windows in his room, bringing in fresh air. A few times he dozes off, then awakens again, his hand reaching out in a panic for my own.

Next week, Nathan and I will go to the courthouse and file the paperwork, and I'll be his wife. His wife. It seems too soon. Less than two weeks ago I was spinning around a pole and picking crumpled dollar bills off beer-stained carpet. Now I sit in a six-hundred-dollar dress, next to my father, just an hour from my mansion.

There is a gentle knock on the door, and Pam comes in.

"I'm sorry, but visitors' hours are ending. We have to start night rounds."

I nod, stretching as I stand, meeting her kind eyes with a grateful smile. "Thank you, Pam. For everything. He speaks so highly of you."

She beams, clasping her hands together before her generous bosom. "He's lucky to have a daughter like you."

I force a smile, and hope it looks authentic. I know what she sees: a devoted daughter, willing to authorize any expense to ensure her father's comfort and well-being. The previous facility knows the truth. They know that he was alone during the first six months of his sickness. They know a lonely old man whose insurance was running out, the one whose daughter didn't bother to visit, or even send flowers. Though that is assuming that they got to know him at all.

I turn away before my smile breaks. I appreciate her false view of me, and the genuine care, love, and attention that this place shows to Dad. Maybe with every visit, the guilt will lessen. I can't make up for six months of neglect. But I can try as hard as I can.

CHAPTER 15

I head out, through the lobby, the desk nurse nodding to me. "Good evening, Ms. Dumont."

"Good evening." I pull on a jacket and move down a long hall, past closed rooms and empty lounges. It smells of clean comfort, the luxury facility one that could easily pass for a spa. My heels echo against the floor, and I nod to a security guard. Fifty steps to my car. Sixty miles to the house. An unknown duration until his hands.

Inside, there is a hard twist of dread, the urge to get in my car and head south instead of north. The emotion makes no sense. In the moments when Nathan has reached for me, I've melted under his touch. I think my dread is more for my heart. With each experience with him, I guard it fiercely. And with each experience, I feel it crack a little more. Tonight, I'm at my weakest emotionally—my heart warm and grateful for the opportunities he has afforded me and my father. Tonight, before I even step in his house, I can feel the warm tendrils of emotion slipping uninvited into my heart.

I push aside the thoughts, and reach for the handle of my new car, a sleek black Mercedes, the car unlocking at my touch. Then, I am inside, the facility's gates opening, and I am heading north.

Drew stands by the front door, glancing at his watch as I step out of the vehicle. "He's been waiting," he says quietly, opening the door as I approach.

"I hit some traffic." I step inside and stop when I see Nathan standing by the large windows, his back to me, his eyes on the city lights, faint in the distance. He's in his customary suit, but has lost the jacket, the sleeves rolled up to his elbows. I glance at Drew, a question in my eyes. His expression gives nothing away, and I set my purse down, passing my keys to Drew.

"Mr. Dumont, I'll park the Missus's car. Will you need me for anything else?"

"Yes." My eyes close briefly at that response. Over half the times that Nathan has fucked me, Drew has been present, a silent observer whose purpose is completely lost on me. I suspect, more than voyeurism, that it has something to do with control. Control is a food that Nathan seems to feed on, devouring it with a vulgarity that clashes with his smooth exterior. What I'm unsure about is if he is manipulating me or Drew in the process. As little as I understand our dynamic, I understand theirs even less. At times they seem friends, then adversaries, then Drew concedes and plays the role of dutiful employee. It's a mindfuck that I want no part of. In the times that Drew's watched us, I can't help but wonder what he is thinking. He feigns disinterest, his head cast to the side or down to the floor in a preoccupied, respectful manner. But sometimes, when my head flips back, or when Nathan suddenly spins me around, I catch his eyes on me. Burning green eyes that pin me in place. And in that fire, in that intense stare, I think I see arousal. I think I see want.

Nathan gestures with a hand to the back lawn. "Wait for me in back. I want to spend some time with Candace, then I'll be there."

From my peripheral vision, I see Drew nod, turning, the door closing, my engine purring a short moment later. He'll take it to the garage. Tomorrow, it will be detailed back to showroom condition. If I've learned anything in these ten days, it is that everything in this house is maintained to perfection. I scrape my freshly painted nails against the front of one thigh. *Including me.*

"How is your father?"

I smile. "He's okay. He is very grateful for the new facility. Thank you for moving him."

"Have they discovered what is wrong with him?"

I swallow. "No."

He turns away from the window, moving to a large leather chair and settling into it, setting his drink on the table. His eyes watch as I move around the couch, stopping before him. I wait for the command, my body tightening, the silk of my panties already beginning to stick between my legs.

"Come here." He slides a little lower in the chair, his head against the white leather, his chin tilted up, blue eyes staring out from chiseled masculinity.

I move closer, his legs coming together, then I am straddling him, my skirt pushed up, his hands reaching around me to pull down the zipper. I lean forward, my fingers loosening his tie, his hands gently gripping my waist, his eyes on mine as my fingers work, neither of us saying anything in this moment.

I love his eyes. They are the only way I can read him. His body gives so little away; he controls his emotions so well. But his eyes are traitorous to his carefully maintained control. They blaze when he is angry, they soften when he is yielding, and they grow heavy with need when he is aroused.

Right now, he is aroused. I don't need his eyes to know that. I can feel it underneath me, straining against the fabric of his dress pants.

His fingers move to the buttons of my cardigan, thumbing the small pearls as he releases them, one by one, his large hands slipping underneath and palming my breasts through the thin fabric of my camisole, the sensation causing a shiver to ripple through me. He yanks at the last button, the pearl popping off, causing a giggle to rise in my throat. Then the silk blend is tossed aside, his hands pulling the cami over my head until it joins the cardigan, and my upper half is bare before him.

"No bra?" he questions, a dark look in his eyes and his hands move, brushing across my nipples, their skin puckering in the cool room.

I shake my head, biting my lower lip, stifling a gasp as his hands grip the weight of me, one breast in each hand, his eyes taking on a gleam of ownership. He pushes with his hands, communicating his desire, and I begin to move my hips, my lace and silk mound grinding over him, my want visible through the fabric.

I need to see more of him, the desire taking over me. My fingers tremble as they move, unbuttoning his shirt, spreading it open so that my hands can explore his skin. I lean forward, lowering my mouth to his hot surface, skimming my tongue and teeth over the hard planes of his chest. His pelvis unexpectedly tilts, pushing me higher until our faces are level, and his mouth is on mine.

I get lost in his kisses. It is where I communicate with him freely, my mouth recklessly pouring out emotions that are best contained. Our tongues have no filter, the heat of our kisses lighting a fire between us that can only be put out with his cock. I reach down, my frantic hands grasping and pulling on leather, clasp, a button and zipper, a concert of hurried motions until I have him in my hand, hard and ready, his skin stretched tight, moisture already present at his tip.

He pulls me down, my hands quickly positioning him beneath me, tugging wet panties aside for his entrance. His mouth reluctantly releases me, his eyes watching me hungrily, fixed on my face as he thrusts up and into me.

I groan at the bare penetration, the thick push of him inside of me, the bare skin against my own, the first thrust almost painful in its stretch. I close my eyes and push fully down, a hiss whistling through his mouth as I rest for a quick moment atop him. My thoughts flicker to Drew and how this must look through the glass walls of the house.

He pulls at my skirt, slipping it over my head and throwing it aside, his hands running through my hair and gripping it tightly, pulling it back so that my neck is exposed.

I lose any thoughts of Drew when his mouth hits my neck, taking a possessive and decadent journey from my jaw to collarbone. His hands and hips lift and pump, a perfect orchestration of rhythm that swiftly takes me up the mountain of orgasm. I dig my nails into his shoulders, letting him take control, the ride one that is exquisite, my orgasm sharp and intense when it comes. He doesn't stop, his breath hard, pumps rapid, until he reaches his peak, his mouth finding mine, one last shuddering thrust delivered.

I collapse against his chest, his heart thudding against my ear. There is the slow drag of his fingers across my back and I sigh, melting into his chest. Then he pats my back in the perfunctory way a doctor might test refluxes.

"I need to go outside."

Of course he does. I roll off of him, swallowing a response, and stand. He doesn't look at me when he stands. Maybe I'm an idiot for expecting that he would.

"I am not signing up for romance, or affection, or a full time job. You should never expect that from me."

I grab my clothes from the floor and head to the bathroom to change.

NATHAN

With Cecile, it had all been such a production. Two wedding planners. A hundred thousand dollars in flowers. Her days had been spent poring over catalogs, in dress fittings, auditioning musicians and writing checks.

All of that bullshit, and look how it had turned out.

He watches the courthouse come into view and turns to Candace. "Let's go."

They wait, sitting on metal folding chairs, then on a wooden bench, and listen to the other couples, each one a depressing Lifetime movie in the making. They were out of place here. His custom suit. Her dark jeans and silk shirt. She fidgets, her hands running along the length of her thighs, and he remembers the ring.

He opens his jacket, reaching into the left side and pulling out the dark velvet box. "Go ahead and put this on." He holds it out to her, and she looks up at him.

Ten thousand dollars of beauty treatments and they couldn't cover up that look. That nervous hope that floods her face and makes him feel like fresh Tennessee shit.

"This is for me?"

He doesn't answer, and she takes the box carefully, as if it holds the Hope diamond. He'd had Mark pick the ring, something appropriate for the Nashville scene, and he watches her eyes widen at the three-carat diamond, one surrounded by emeralds, and its accompanying band. He looks away, and thinks of Cecile, the night he had proposed, the way she had screamed so loudly that everyone in Tahiti

89

must have heard.

She pulls at the rings, fumbling with them, and he takes the box, removing the rings and reaching for her hand. "Here." He slides them on, and doesn't miss the small hitch in her breath, the lift of her eyes, and there is a minor moment between them in a day when he wanted no moment at all.

"I can't believe we're getting married," she whispers.

He releases her hand, snapping the ring box closed with quick efficiency, and pulling his own simple band from the pocket of his jacket, looking up to the judge and willing their names to be called.

CHAPTER 16

As a girl, I always pictured my wedding. I stab a gold-tined fork into week old cake and lift it to my lips. This was never what I had in mind.

"Hold it right there!" A voice calls out. "Now smile!"

I obey, and there is the flash of bulbs, my vision gone for a moment, then the dots clear and I can see again. I drop the smile, setting down my fork, and look up. "What's next?"

"Let's get a shot of you two dancing." The man strides forward, his heels clicking across on the floor. He stops before a large backdrop, one that shows a stone balcony, vineyards behind it, with a peek of ocean in the corner.

I lift up the skirt of my gown, one that I swooned over thirty minutes ago and now absolutely hate, everything about this experience slicing my innards to bits. A reception shouldn't be staged, the wedding dress rented, the love added via photoshop. I stop in the midst of the set and stare at the backdrop, a crease running along it's outside edge. "It looks fake."

"It won't. Just wait till you see these photos. You'll be *amazed*." He snaps his fingers at Nathan, who looks up from his phone with a bored yawn. Two hours into this marriage, and I already want to strangle my husband.

We get into place, our position orchestrated by the photographer's assistant, a spotlight added to perfect the image. Someone in the background hums, and we attempt a few steps.

"STOP!" the man shrieks. "God, you'd think you've never danced before. Just stay in place and look in love."

Look in love. As if it is a simple request. I lift my gaze to Nathan and fight the urge to cry. He looks down at me, and his face changes, his brows tightening, eyes softening with what I almost believe to me concern. He cups my face and I feel the wet embarrassment of a tear.

"What's wrong?" he says gruffly.

"That's PERFECT!" the man crows, the rapid shutter of his camera clicking. "Now, kiss her!"

I close my eyes, another tear falling, Nathan's hand lifting my chin, his lips soft against mine, and against his kiss, I swallow a sob.

CHAPTER 17

Boredom is a dangerous bitch, one that gives credence to idle thoughts, and gives legs to dangerous ideas. In my fourth week at Nathan's, boredom has become item number one on my daily agenda.

My days are melding together, a constant cycle of working out, make up, hair, and boredom. I eat prepackaged meals. Wear preselected outfits. Dutifully move through a routine barked at me by a hundred pound pit bull. When I'm not attending to my physical health and appearance, I nap. Read. Sit and wait for the sound of Nathan's car. Occasionally, we go to business dinners with his investors—long meals in five-star restaurants where I eat quietly and am mostly ignored.

Some nights he doesn't return. I sit in the guesthouse with the doors open so that I'll hear his engine. I keep the television on low, a magazine or book ignored in my hands. If he doesn't return by eight, I eat. At ten, I close the doors and curtains. I'm just another employee of the house, all of us here to serve a purpose. Drew: security. Mark: details. Me … I am still figuring that one out. Orgasm deliverer? Comedic relief? Charity case?

This weekend we are going to Napa with some of his friends and their wives. I'm embarrassed at how excited I am for the trip. Rosit Fenton has already come by, my wardrobe restocked, my hair touched up, a fresh wax job performed. The trip is part of some sort of charity event we are attending, and Rosit gave me a crash course on dining etiquette, along with backgrounds on all of the attending individuals. He also provided me with a false background of my own, something close enough to the truth so that I am less likely to screw it up. Prior to meeting Nathan, I was an event planner, from Destin. We met at a club one night. Had a whirlwind weekend and instantly fell in love. I've practiced answers from every possible scenario, and I'm still terrified over their questions. Not too terrified not to attend, mind you. I've been counting down the days to get out of this house.

"Are you coming with us to Napa?" I sit at the kitchen island, and munch on a carrot.

"No." Drew's answer, as typical, barely tells me anything.

"He's not really in *danger*, is he?"

Drew regards me carefully from his place by the fridge. "What do you mean?"

"You're supposed to be his security, right?" I hop off the stool and walk to the fridge, pulling open the door and searching for some bit of yumminess that Beth might have overlooked.

"Among other things."

"So if he's in danger, then who's protecting him right now?"

"Mark's with him."

I roll my eyes. "I know that Mark is *with* him, but Mark isn't exactly intimidating." Mark's the type you'd call when you wanted to dump a body, and needed a well-researched, well-thought-out plan. Put him in a dangerous situation, and I'm pretty sure he'd pull out a calculator, toss it at your head, and run.

"Are you done eating? You should return to the guesthouse."

"Stop calling it the guesthouse." I push aside a gallon of carrot juice, making a face at the soy milk behind it.

"Okay, time to return to *your* house."

"Why can't I stay here? Why do I have to be locked away in there all day?" I grab a bottled water and shut the fridge, twisting off the cap as I prop one hip against the island. "Nathan works in development, right? Hotels, apartment complexes?"

He says nothing, and my boredom takes the opportunity to run free. "Development isn't dangerous. And half the time, he doesn't even lock the front door."

"Your point?"

I shrug, taking a swig. "Just seems like you are expendable."

"Let me worry about that."

"And what's with making me sleep outside? Why can't I hang out in the house during the day? Or sleep in his room?"

"Do you *want* to sleep with him?"

His tone gives me pause, and I set the bottle on the counter. "It'd be nice not to sleep alone."

I intended the comment to be lighthearted, a flippant response that would be ignored. But he says nothing, and an awkward silence stretches between us. I pick at the label on my water. "How long have you worked for Nathan?"

He crosses his arms and shoots me a pained look. "Why the sudden questions?"

I crunch happily on a carrot in a way that I know he will find exasperating. "Answer one of them, and I'll go on my little way like a good girl."

"Which one?"

I grab a fresh handful of orange sticks. "Is he really in any danger?"

"Wealthy men are always in danger. Now, *move.*" He ends the order with some form of a snarl, emphasizing the last word and unfolding his arms, as if he'll force me from the kitchen.

I laugh, sticking a new carrot into my mouth and bumping my hip against him as I round the island and head to my prison. "Fine ... but your answer sucked. I'll get you with a better question tomorrow."

He glowers at me, a look that would have terrified me a month ago. Now, it only causes me to beam, the brief bit of human interaction well worth the sexy death stare.

I push open the heavy glass door and step onto the sunlight-filled deck.

CHAPTER 18

I need a hobby. The marital agreement states that I can have one, as long as it doesn't interfere with my wifely duties. Nathan's schedule seems to reliably keep him out of the house from nine to five, eight hours open for whatever random hobby I should decide to engage in. It shouldn't be that difficult for me to find a hobby that will fit during that window. The agreement also states that I may have friends, but unless I stalk strangers at Starbucks, it's going to be pretty hard to find those.

Last weekend, we flew to Napa. Nathan was mobbed the moment our plane landed, men and women alike flocking to his side, pulling on his arm, whispering into his ear, and laughing at his jokes. I had been so worried about our stiff exchanges, but he transformed before my eyes, an easy grin stretching across his face, a casual and affable elegance his new façade. I was shocked, my jaw literally dropping as I stared at the mystery who was anyone but my husband.

He maintained this exterior for three days straight, entertaining scores of society blue bloods, telling stories I have never heard, and bidding on extravagant auction items, his arm draped lovingly around my shoulder. He planted soft kisses on my neck in the presence of others and ran his fingers lightly over my arm as if he couldn't touch me enough. I saw the glances, the swoons from other woman. *She is so lucky. They are so in love.* They didn't know the truth. That when he would lean in and whisper in my ear his words were anything but romantic. *Stop fidgeting. Uncross your legs. Sit up straight.* I behaved, I smiled, I made the proper social gestures, and said the correct things. I beamed at Nathan, laughed at his stories, and accepted his loving gestures as if they were normal. And in the evenings, when the door to our two-bedroom suite closed, he would reward me. On the soft bed, against the wall, in the shower. On my back, on my knees, standing, and with his mouth. When you subtracted his whispered orders, the separate bedrooms, and the false exteriors, it was the best weekend of my life.

We returned four days ago, the plane landing with a soft bump that woke me from my nap. I stretched and smiled over at Nathan, glancing out the window and seeing the familiar hangers, the arched display of the airport. "We home?"

He nodded without looking at me, unbuckling his belt and moving to the front. That was Sunday, and we haven't spoken since. The first day, I dismissed it as nothing, my weekend high keeping a smile on my face, a bounce in my step. Drew watched me closely that day, his eyes narrowed, his gaze wary. The second day I began to wonder if something was wrong. Now, on day four, it seems clear. I am being punished for something.

I check my watch. 9:04 AM. Nathan should have left by now. I stand up and slide open the glass door, stepping out on the pool deck.

His hard glare pins me in the doorway as soon as I step into the main house. He stands in the kitchen, the island between us, six feet of gorgeous constrained by a custom suit. I can see the anger in his eyes, his face turning into a scowl as he mutters something to Drew. Drew makes a sharp gesture with his head, the message clear, and I step backward, pulling the door closed, the summer heat settling around me like a hot, scratchy sweater. I stand there for a moment. *Bad Candace. Get out, Candace.*

Anger seeps through me. *Why is he so difficult? Am I that irritating, my mere presence that unbearable to his peace of mind?* My clothes, the proper blend of luxury and sex, are suddenly thick and constricting, the tight wool-blend top ridiculous in the summer humidity. I feel a sudden surge of recklessness, pushed by the wave of hot claustrophobia that seizes my entire body. I yank at the sleeveless turtleneck, pulling it over my head, feeling a moment of euphoria when the hot fabric hits the white pavers. My skirt follows, one quick zip down. I stare at my nude thigh-high lace stockings, clipping to the bottom of La Perla garters. There's no need for stockings in June, they had been slid on in the pathetic hope that he might, on this day, grant me a session with his cock. I slip out of my heels, and roll the expensive sheer fabric down my legs, flipping my head up to find him and Drew staring at me through the glass, an expression of horror on Drew's face. Nathan simply watches, a cold look of disinterest in his eyes. *Oh, look. There is my wife. Throwing a temper tantrum in front of the staff.*

I stare into his eyes, my body covered by only a sheer shelf bra and a barely existent thong. I can only hope my eyes communicate the fury radiating through my body, my hurt at his neglect, at his snub of me and the corner of his world that I inhabit. Then, I dive.

The water shocks me. I am forbidden from the pool, my hair stylist repeatedly preaching the harm that chlorine will cause to my now-expensive tresses. Nathan agreed, adding a new rule to my long list. *No swimming.* So I am unprepared for its cool embrace, the smooth grip of moisture that instantly refreshes my sticky skin, sliding bubbles across my surface. I come up for air, the sun's heat suddenly friendly and warm on my face, tickling me as it slides droplets of water off my face. Then I duck back into the underwater world and don't come up for quite some time.

I swim laps until my muscles cramp, ache, and then cramp again. I am filled with glee at my insubordination, my first act of rebellion incredible in its release. The water cools my aggression, my hatred, my anger toward the black beauty that is Nathan. At the end of each lap, on my backward spin, I peer through the clear water, my eyes searching for a body at the edge of the pool, someone who will admonish me, order me to get out of the pool, perhaps even Nathan. But lap after lap, no one is there, and so I continue. I swim until I am gasping for breath, my heart thudding against my chest, my legs and arms deliciously exhausted.

I drag myself from the water, lying back on the warm pavers of the pool deck, my eyes closing, a smile crossing my features. Nathan would find some way to punish me, perhaps more coldness, more nights where I fall asleep waiting for his call. But this act, this childish strip down and swim, was worth it. I needed the moment of backbone—at a time when I feel I'm losing all the pieces of myself.

There, in the warm sun, my skin and lingerie drying out above tired muscles, my exhausted body relaxes, and under the dark stare of Nathan, I fall asleep.

CHAPTER 19

I am in my bathroom, towel-drying my hair, when Drew speaks.

"Mr. Dumont is requesting you."

The sudden words startle me, and I turn and glare at him. "Can't you knock?"

He says nothing, his hands in his pockets, and I lean forward, returning to my task. Strange, for Nathan to still be home in the middle of the day, and sending Drew for me. He has never requested me for anything but sex. After four days of ignoring me, I break a rule, and a half hour later, he asks for me.

"Mr. Dumont—"

"I know. Is requesting me." I stand, shaking out my hair and tossing the towel toward the basket. "Should I get dressed?"

His eyes travel over my silk robe, cinched at the waist over nothing but me, the fabric sticking to my skin, still wet from my after-swim shower. "No. I'm sure that will be fine."

I nod, passing by him and toward the door, butterflies starting a nervous dance in my belly.

In the background, the roar of a weed eater begins.

***

"You needed me?" I stop in the doorway, watching him turn from the bar, his expression dark.

He nods to the pool. "What the fuck was that? Are you five years old? Are temper tantrums going to be your standard communication tool?"

I flush. He's right. I should have stepped back inside. Confronted him with my feelings. Or swallowed it all and retained my dignity. I slide the door shut behind me, and without the sounds of the landscapers, the room is too quiet. "You're right. I'm upset at you. And I should have just spoken to you about it."

He steps closer, his jaw flexing, and when he stops before me, I'm reminded of how much of a man he is. His scent. His build, the suit tight to his muscles. His height, towering above my flats. "You're upset at *me*?" He laughs, cruel and incredulously, and anger flares in me.

"Yes," I grit out. "You've given me the cold shoulder since we returned from Napa. You ignore me and look at me with ..." I search for an appropriate word. "Disdain." I finish. "As if I'm—"

I lose track of my thoughts when he grabs me, his hands tight on my forearms, my robe's thin silk doing nothing to prevent what will be bruises. I look at him in panic.

The controlled version of him is gone, his face a mask of barely restrained emotion; his breath is coming in short bursts, his expression dark. He drags me forward, pushes me onto the leather chaise lounge, until I am on my back and he is towering over me, his hands in fists.

"Nathan, please," I gasp, moving away from him, my robe open around my legs.

"You think this is a game?" he hisses. "Our marriage, our agreement?"

I open my mouth, searching for something to say, not understanding his anger. Is this our marriage? I ask a question, I voice my feelings, and unleash *this*?

He leans closer, until his mouth is inches from mine, his breath hot on my skin. "Answer me."

I wet my lips. "No," I whisper.

"No, what?" he snarls, yanking the sash on my robe, the silk moving easily under his strength.

"No, it's not a game." I keep my face timid, my voice soft, but inside my teeth bare and my claws flex. No, it's *not* a game; this is my *life*, my worth, my sanity. For a man who doesn't like games, he should throw out the rules and stop keeping score. His eyes are hard on mine and I've never seen him this angry—didn't know he was capable of this level of emotion at all. I should be scared, but a thrill of excitement courses through me at the presence of life in him.

He reaches forward, gripping the back of my neck and pulling me up, pressing his mouth roughly to mine as he pulls open my robe, baring my body to him. It's not a kiss. It's a domination—strong movements of his tongue that torment my mouth. He nips my bottom lip, fucks me with his tongue, then gently kisses my swollen lips, taking one final journey of my mouth before he pulls off.

I open my eyes, expecting a softer Nathan above me, expecting the change in his kiss to reflect the forgiveness that had occurred. His fists have loosened, those hands now running rampant over my body, my robe fully open, my legs parted with his knee. His face has calmed, the deep lines faded, the set of his mouth relaxed. But his eyes betray him. His eyes show the fierce anger that still burns brightly. I still don't know why he's mad, or what I've done wrong, but I understand one thing—my punishment just changed. I didn't want to be ignored, and now that table is being yanked out from beneath me.

His eyes flick to the backyard, then return to me, and I understand. This is how he will punish me—putting me on display while he fucks me senseless. He will remind me of where I came from, treat me like the whore that I—that one night—was.

And he does. "Stand. Go to the window."

He puts my palms to the glass, my breasts stiffening in the cool air, his hands taking a generous tour of them as he settles in behind me, the soft brush of his dress pants soon replaced by the bare touch of his thighs, the erect press of his cock.

"Lift your head." He almost pants the words, his hands settling on my ass cheeks, and digging into the sore muscles there. I resist, my head hung, hating the craving of my body, the need that thrums through me. He leans forward, and he gathers my damp hair, fisting it and pulling back, lifting my head, my world blurring as the backyard comes into focus. On the far side of the pool, a landscaper stands, the hedge clippers hanging limply and forgotten in his hands. Our eyes meet, and he flushes, looking away, his hands tightening on the handles of the tool.

The shame fades, replaced by something unexpected—a fresh shot of arousal. I glance over, to the second man, one who walks along the edge of the pool deck, his head down, focused on the weed-eater in his hands. Any moment, he will realize what is happening. Any moment, he will look over and see me, bent forward and naked, being fucked by my—I gasp when Nathan pushes inside, the shove of penetration so hard that my breasts bounce from the impact. He releases my hair and there is the hard sting of his hand against my ass, his words spitting out hard and unforgiving, "If I want to ignore you, I will. And if I want to enjoy you, I will. You belong to *me*. You are mine."

I claw against the glass, my breath catching as he slaps the area again, the slow drag of his cock outward conflicting with the violent push of it back inside.

"Nathan," I gasp. I don't even know what I'm trying to say. *Don't stop? More? Please?* My mind is too scattered to form sentences and too confused with my arousal to know anything but that I am loving every motherfucking moment of this.

He reaches forward, his legs settling against mine, his body curving over the bend of mine as he slides his palms around my ribs and closes his hands around my breasts.

I moan from the sensation, the hard squeeze of his hands, the possessive growl that comes from his throat and vibrates against the back of my neck. "I love your fucking breasts," he swears, kneading them together. "God, I fucking love them."

I open my eyes at the admission, catching the wide-eyed gaze of the second landscaper, then Nathan is yanking me around, pulling my face to his, his lips rough against mine.

Are they still watching? Do they see when he pushes me to my knees, his hand firm on my head, my bare body before his clothed one? They probably watch when I take his cock deep down my throat, my body shaking from the effort, when my back contracts and I gag.

They see when his legs flex, his head drops back, and he fills my throat with satisfaction.

He's twisted. To do that to me, to come with the knowledge that we have an audience. I'm ashamed that I played along, that I didn't twist out of his grip and run back to my room. I'm ashamed that, at the height of it, when I felt their eyes, and hated Nathan's demands, I was aroused. Aching in my pussy, moisture dripping down my leg, aroused. I moaned when he spanked me. I begged for more as he fucked me. I looked into his eyes and all but asked for his cum.

Maybe I'm as twisted as he is.

CHAPTER 20

Our agreement states that sex will only be asked for once a day, today's quota already filled. Nathan is a man of regulations, our agreement one that he follows to the letter. Still, I dress in expectation of his return from the office. It is silly, vain hopes that a simple clothing change will recapture some normalcy in a day that has already gone so wrong.

I hear the growl of Nathan's car, and swallow, sitting before the vanity and running a brush over my hair. I pull at the top drawer, unveiling the black velvet, the delicate jewelry laid out in neat order. Gently running my fingers over the line of earrings, I select a pair of pearls. I hear the sound of the door and I look up, into the mirror.

Drew enters, wandering along the bed, his eyes moving over the neatly made coverlet, the dark television, the vase of fresh flowers. It's a far cry from the cramped and messy bedroom in Dibs' house. Maybe it's because I still feel like a guest, or maybe cleaning is my new hobby, but it is—as always—spotless.

He stops a step or two behind me, and meets my eyes in the mirror. "Are you okay?"

I glance to the house, nodding, Nathan's frame absent from my view of the great room. Drew reaches forward, his hand startling me, and fingers the end of my hair, examining its dark chocolate strands. "I like it dark."

I only nod, surprised at his nearness, at the warm hesitancy in his eyes. *So do I.* I had spent last night flipping through Rosit's 'before' images in my beauty book, and had almost winced at the bleach blonde images of me. I'd been a back tattoo and droopy cigarette away from white trash. Now, looking back in the mirror, at the expensive reflection of myself—I can barely match the two images. On the outside, I am completely different. Inside, I'm still a stripper, trading my body for security.

He clears his throat. "Earlier today, what happened ... none of them could see. The afternoon light casts a reflective glare on the windows."

I don't respond. His lie rests in the space between us. I'm the one who sits in this glass house, who stares into that great room and waits for his figure to appear. Reflection has never been a problem. "Are you here to fetch me?"

He nods, and my stomach tightens at the news.

I fasten the second pearl earring. "Do I look okay?"

He steps back, releasing my hair. The skin around his mouth changes, his five o'clock shadow stretching around a tight smile. "You look beautiful," he says finally. "Like always. Nathan will be pleased."

I push back from the vanity and stand, willing this memory from my mind: his concern, his proximity, his touch on my hair, his lies for my sanity. I don't really give a fuck if Nathan is pleased. Half of me is still upset over his earlier outburst, the other half is still aroused.

I walk to the house, feeling Drew's eyes on me, his hand settling on my back as he reaches forward and opens the door. "Mr. Dumont is in the office."

The office. I raise my eyebrows. I haven't seen the office since my first tour of the house, everything off limits except for the common areas and gym. I follow Drew's lead and step into the room, a big space with dark blue walls and deep wood accents. Nathan is there, standing by the window, his tie loosened, arms crossed over his chest. I stop.

"Swimming. How important is it to you?"

I try to hide my surprise. This may be the first time Nathan has ever asked my opinion on something, our conversations limited to instructions and orders. I look down, searching for the right words. "Not important enough for me to negotiate for, but I would enjoy swimming. It would give me something to do during the day."

"My issue, my anger earlier today, was not about you swimming." He steps forward, rolling up one sleeve in perfect, precise folds, unveiling muscular forearms. "Granted, I *was* upset that you purposely disobeyed my rule—the rules are in place for a reason, and I need you to follow them. But what caused me to lose my temper was your stripping down to your underwear in front of Drew."

My face flushes, and I wonder where Drew is right now, if he is still behind me, or if he just dropped me off and moved on.

"I understand that you have trouble understanding the difference between our sex and your exhibitionism, so know *this*: unless I tell you to, you will stay fully clothed in front of the staff. Do you understand?"

I nod meekly, my cheeks burning as I am talked to in the manner someone would a small child.

"I'll speak with your hair stylist. I'm sure there is some product that can be purchased to protect your hair. I will allow you to swim, assuming you do it during the day when I am at work." He finishes the second sleeve, both forearms now bare, the look—combined with his loose tie and rumpled hair—incredibly hot.

I will allow you to swim. His gifts are still insults. "Thank you," I say stiffly. "But I still don't know why you seem so mad at me."

He raises his eyebrows, looking at me as if I am a dolt. "I just explained that to you."

"No," I struggle to explain. "I meant before. Before I stripped down in front of Drew. Ever since we got back from Napa, you've acted as if I've messed up in some way. Was it something that happened in Napa?"

NATHAN

"Was it something that happened in Napa?"

She asks the question so cluelessly, as if Napa Valley had been fun and games, and not a torture chamber of temptation.

Yes, he wants to scream. *Yes, it has to do with Napa. I don't love you. I am using you, and everything that happened in Napa felt like fraud.* He swallows. "It has nothing to do with Napa except that I feel you came back from that trip with unrealistic expectations about our relationship."

She crosses her arms over her chest, and the air between them turns cold. "So you thought you'd be a grade A asshole to push me back into my corner?"

"Possibly." He lifts his chin, returning the glare that she slings in his direction. "And from the look you're giving me, I think I've accomplished that purpose."

She snorts. "Don't flatter yourself. You can be a human being without having a woman fall for you."

Isn't that the truth. He'd been more than human with Cecile, and look how that had ended.

"All I'm asking is that you not be cruel."

He can't give her that. It's not in him to be kind and not care. It's too risky to befriend her when she is only a tool. And this backbone that she's growing isn't helping anything. He jerks a head toward the door. "I think it's time you went back to your room."

If a glare could be tangible, hers would slice his head off. She waits, and there is a moment when he almost expects her to refuse, to stand her ground and just stare him down until the mosquitos came out and Drew nodded off from the pure boredom of it all.

But she doesn't. She turns on one sexy heel, giving him a parting look at that deliciously round ass, and heads out the door, the scent of her perfume lingering as she all but stomped toward her room

CHAPTER 21

"Your husband is so handsome."

I look up from my book, my feet tucked beneath me, my father's snores comforting in their regularity. "I'm sorry?"

Pam beams, a worn *Southern Life* magazine clutched in her hands, as she scurries closer. "Jeanie brought this in, it's got photos from your trip to Napa. I didn't realize how handsome your husband was. Why, you're famous!"

She unfolds the magazine, folding it back on itself, thrusting the glossy pages forward, one bare fingernail tapping insistently on the page. I accept it carefully, my eyes devouring the pages.

I know that Nathan is important, a part of Nashville society, which apparently makes him fodder for southern gossip rags. I glance quickly through the photos, ones from a charity luncheon we attended, grapevines in the distance, the sunny warmth of the day coming through in the images. The shots seem to focus on us, the other couples in attendance mostly ignored by the photographer. I look fabulous—glowing with happiness, my head tilted toward Nathan, a proud smile on his face, as he looks at me with an emotion some might confuse with love. My hand tightens on the magazine. I love these pages; I want to pore over each one, to savor the images I wish were real.

My chair shifts as Pam's weight rests on its arm, her bosom against my arm as she leans forward and points to a photo of the two of us. "This is my favorite one of him. Whew!" She fans herself dramatically. "What I wouldn't give to trade places with you, honey." She laughs, a pleasant trill of joy.

"Can I hold on to this? I'd like to show it to Dad when he wakes up."

"Certainly." She pats my shoulder, heaving to her feet and stepping over to his bed, checking his monitors and recording in his chart. It is one of the things I appreciate about this place. His records are kept clean, orderly, his blood work easy to read, his tests occurring when they should, according to schedule. That alone is a Godsend, never mind the daily delivery of fresh flowers, the delicious food, or the endless patience of the doctors. There are only sixteen patients in this entire complex. Sixteen patients tended to by five doctors, twelve nurses, and a round-the-clock support staff. Here he is a name, not a number. And here, he is actually getting better.

They still don't know what is wrong. But they have been able to determine what helps. He is on a cocktail of drugs and antibiotics and is slowly responding, the digital figures on his charts improving. And slowly, tentatively, I am beginning to have hope.

He wakes at two pm, watching me before I am aware of it. I glance over, surprised to see his peaceful stare, a smile on his face. I set aside my book, standing and stepping to his side, placing a soft kiss on his cheek before adjusting his bed. "How you feeling, Dad? Are you in any pain?"

He shakes his head. "I'm good, Candace. Sit down. They fuss over me enough already."

I hold out a cup of water, waiting until he takes a sip before I sit.

"What are you reading?"

I hold up the book. "John Grisham."

"I thought you would have read all of his by now."

I grin. "I have, but I'm out of material. This one's a loaner from Pam. I'm going to swing by the bookstore tomorrow to get a fresh stack."

"What's that?" He points to the magazine, still open on the table. I stand, folding over the page, and pass it to him.

He studies the pictures, glancing up at me. "This is from your trip a couple of weeks ago?"

"Yeah, when we went to California."

I'm not sure what I expect. Admiration at the article, at Nathan's success, at the staged photos of our happiness? My father has been less than enthusiastic at my announcement of a husband. I waited until my second visit to spring it on him, waiting until after the courthouse ceremony in case something fell through. I had gushed about Nathan, creating a picture of a faithful and loving husband. I think he's hurt that Nathan hasn't visited, didn't ask him for my hand in marriage, hasn't made any effort whatsoever at a relationship. So maybe these photos will help to support my façade and soothe his concerns.

I don't expect the magazine to be carefully set down, a sharp pinch to his features when he turns to me. "And you're happy, Care Bear?"

The childhood nickname causes my throat to stick, tears pricking the corners of my eyes. A sudden urge swells, one that almost causes my mouth to open, and the raw, unfiltered truth to come out. I swallow hard, smiling brightly, and instead of the clean, smooth flow of truth, dirty, filthy lies spew out.

CHAPTER 22

Nathan is gorgeous. Rich. The best I've ever had in bed. Other than being a supreme pain in the ass, there's no reason why women aren't tripping over themselves to marry the guy. He shouldn't need a contract and financial bribe in order to get a wife.

I think through the logic as Beth takes me through deadlifts, then squats, then lunges. By the time she finishes, I'm drenched in sweat and convinced that something is amiss.

I give her a half-hearted wave goodbye and stumble to the kitchen, the cool blast of refrigerator air tempting. I resist the urge, closing the door, a Voss in hand. I straighten at the sound of footsteps. Twisting off the water bottle's cap, I step sideways, stopping Drew on his path through the kitchen. "I've been thinking…"

He sighs, his steps halting, and he moves back a pace. Weeks ago, it would have offended me. Now, I'm used to the constant readjustment of distance, the wariness in his eyes, as if I'm dangerous, a threat just waiting to implode.

"Nathan wanted a wife. Why?"

"It doesn't matter."

Three words that raise my suspicions even higher.

"Is it a citizenship thing?" I step closer, tilting back the bottle, chugging a sip of cool water, and his eyes move briefly to my neck, then back to my face.

"No. Stop asking questions, Candy."

"Some inheritance requirement? I read a book about that once, where

117

the guy had to get married before he was forty. Or..." I widen my eyes. "I read once that wives don't have to testify against their husbands. Is he planning some sort of—"

My bottle hits the floor, water splashing against my legs as he grips my shoulders, slamming the refrigerator door closed and shoving me against it, his face close to mine. I tense, my eyes darting to his furious green ones, taking a quick gasp of air before closing my mouth.

"Shut up," he whispers, the words a growl against my skin. I realized so many things in one brief second—his hard body against my own, the unforgiving ridge of his muscles impressive and rough against my damp clothing. The peppermint flavor of his breath, hot in my ear, yet finding its way to my nose, and I inhale his scent—a blend of grass and sweat and mint that is intoxicating.

His hands, originally against my shoulders, have moved. One now cups my neck, pulling my head to one side, the other grips my ass, his large hand slipping under the loose hem of my shorts and grips my bare skin tightly against him, fitting our bodies together in one unending connection.

His breath, that hot air that was against my ear, moves along the curve of my neck, his head lowering to my skin, his breaths quickening to match the fast beats of his heart, which thud hard against my breasts.

Oh, and *that arousal.* Hard and hot, a brand against my leg, my body twisting underneath his hands in order to put that arousal where it belongs, tight against my sex, the thin material of my shorts doing nothing but increasing the pleasure when I involuntarily grind against him.

He swears, his hand forcing my head to straighten, his mouth hesitating over mine.

I need it. I need it for no other reason than that I am bored, and he is here, a man who seems so simple compared to Nathan, so basic in his wary distance, his wandering eyes. I need his lips on mine, need that hard cock in more places than against the silk of my shorts. I grind again, one small movement that confirms the size of his need. He groans, and his hand tightens on my ass, pulling me against his cock as he thrusts against me.

His mouth makes the final move and closes the distance, his kiss almost desperate when it collides with my lips.

My heart pounds, body strums, and my brain screams in protest. Then Drew pushes off me, stepping back, and the moment is broken.

We stare at each other, the distance between the island and the fridge too small, our bodies too close. I must look like a mad woman—my hair wild from his hand, eyes needy, mouth panting. He stares at me as if he's afraid, his hands gripping the granite of the counter's edge, his chest heaving. He suddenly moves, holding up his hands and moving slowly away. "Just … Fuck! Just stop asking questions. Please." He moves away, and a moment later, a door slams in his wing of the house.

I worked at Sammy's for three years. You'd think that length of time spent before men, gauging their level of arousal, would have taught me something—maybe the difference between harmless flirting and a danger zone. It would have given me enough experience to steer me in a direction other than the one I am in right now, which *definitely* feels like danger.

My hands shake. I hold them before me, staring at the tremor. I sink to the kitchen floor, picking up my water bottle, my tennis shoes slipping through the slick pool of water. I finish off the remaining amount, waiting for my heart to calm. I need to get to my room, need to separate myself from him, from this kitchen, from the freaking smell of Nathan that always lingers in this house. I need to take a shower, to lie down. I stumble to my feet, shoving the water bottle into the trash, and focus on putting one foot ahead of the other. I make it to the door and then to the deck, two questions dominating my mind, possibly the most dangerous ones of all.

What if Nathan finds out?

What if it happens again?

CHAPTER 23

8:30 AM. The phone rings. It's a foreign sound, Drew or Mark typically walking over if anything is needed. I set down the toothbrush, scooping a mouthful of water into my mouth, and hurriedly rinse. Spitting into the sink, I hurry to the desk, and pick up the receiver. "Hello?"

"Mr. Dumont would like to leave in fifteen minutes. Will you be ready?" Drew's voice is cold and efficient.

"He wants me to go with him?"

"Yes."

I hesitate, looking down at my outfit, a Rosit Fenton ensemble. Cropped silk pants and a cardigan set. Bland boredom, which Nathan seems to prefer. "I'll be there shortly."

I hesitate in the moment before I open the door, seeing him through the glass, in the dining room, a dark figure in navy. Does he know about Drew? Is this about my father? Where could we be going? I step into the cool confines of the house, holding my head high, fighting to keep my features relaxed. He has a phone to his ear, his words low, and he turns at my entrance, his gaze drifting over me. He nods in approval, and a stab of irritation hits me. Will we ever be the couple that hangs out in sweat pants and pajamas? Will he ever crack a joke, or even a smile? Will I ever see Napa Valley Nathan in the privacy of our home?

He waves his hand, beckoning me to follow, and we step into the bright sunlight of the front drive, where Drew and the Maybach await.

The Maybach. I am surprised, the limo our typical vehicle, the Maybach used when Drew and Nathan are alone. I arch my eyebrow at Drew as he opens my car door.

"Guess it's not *that* kind of trip, princess."

I hope my quick entrance into the car hides my flush. Nathan does typically use the space of the limo to satisfy his sexual needs. In retrospect, maybe that's the only reason we take the limo. We certainly don't need that much space.

In the back of the Maybach, Nathan seems too close, the area not large enough for his ego and my nerves. I clasp my hands in my lap, cross my ankles, and try to relax.

Nathan ends his call and glances at me. "I have to go to the courthouse to sign some documents. I thought we could kill two birds with one stone and get your new identification."

I nod, our marriage ceremony completed over a month ago. "I don't have any of the paperwork with me."

"Mark has everything we'll need."

Of course he does. Mark seems to walk around with every piece of paper anyone might possibly want. He knows the caloric content of french fries, historical weather patterns, and every maitre d' and city official in Nashville. It's creepy how smart he is, the gift softened by his complete inability to carry on a coherent conversation. I tried to chat with him at a red light once, and somehow ended up hearing him recite pi to fifty-two decimal places.

Nathan gets on the phone, and I settle into the seat.

***

We leave the courthouse two hours later; my name officially changed, a shiny new driver's license in hand, one that screamed CANDACE DUMONT in giant block letters. It is crazy, but looking at that license, I finally realized what I've done. Married a stranger. Given up on true love. Sold my future in exchange for financial security and a few orgasms a week. I tighten my hands on my license to keep them from shaking.

"I'm hungry. Let's get something to eat, and then Drew can drop me at the office and take you home." Nathan leans forward, his hand wrapping around my knee. I unzip my purse, shoving the license in with fingers that only barely tremble.

I force a smile. "Lunch sounds good."

In the mirror, Drew's eyebrows knit in something akin to worry.

CHAPTER 24

Nathan is in the best mood I have seen him in. Unlike the forced happiness that we adopt in front of the cameras, his exuberance seems genuine, his kind looks and loving smile painless in their delivery. We sit outside; he orders margaritas and beams at me across the table, his smile infectious, my own mouth curving in a bewildered response.

"Candace Dumont," he says the name in wonder, leaning forward and gripping my hand, staring at the stone there. "We should go somewhere and celebrate. Take the honeymoon we never took."

The honeymoon we never took? I take a sip of water, hoping that the alcohol is on its way, wondering who this man is and what he has done with my serious, all-business husband. "A honeymoon?" I can't think of a more creative response.

His grin weakens a little, and he shrugs. "The press would enjoy a honeymoon. Plus, I have business in the Caribbean. You're coming."

I am able to mask my irritation with the arrival of our drinks. I sip the margarita, and glance around the restaurant. I shouldn't be irritated. I should be grateful for the trip, for an opportunity to go somewhere with this beautiful man. The mention of press means photos. Photos mean charismatic Nathan, loving smiles, and soft caresses. Photos mean a weekend like Napa—a weekend that will break my heart in its perfection. "When will we go?"

"Next month. I have a land deal that I need to close first. Once that's taken care of, I will be able to take a couple of days off. Plus, it will take some time to get you a passport." He picks up the menu. "I'll have Drew make the arrangements."

I want to ask if Drew will be joining us, but worry the question will seem odd. Instead, I settle into silence, placing my order, and saying little else.

It's the first meal we have shared without others present. We've had a couple of double dates—arranged for business purposes—dates on which Nathan was on his best behavior. More common has been group outings—a party, a dinner, a tour of a new development, charity events. Group outings are easy for us, the crowds allowing us to mask our limited knowledge of each other, our lack of inside jokes, pet names, and shared history. For some couples, silence is comfortable, everything already discussed, shared, communication possible without speaking. For us, silence is all we have ever known. I do not speak because I don't know what to say. He doesn't speak because he has no interest in talking.

**

"Does Nathan talk to you?" I am tucked into the backseat of the Maybach, staring into eyes in the rearview mirror. It's the first question I've asked him since the kiss. It's funny how I now consider questions dangerous behavior.

His brow furrows. "Talk?"

This is new—an opening to discussion, something out of the ordinary for Drew. I lean forward. "You guys spend a lot of time together. With me, he is always quiet. Does he talk to you?"

"Yes. We've known each other a long time." His eyes are now straight ahead.

A long time. That prompts a stack of new questions in my mind. I mull over them, trying to decide which is most important, which he is most likely to answer. Then he speaks, the question surprising me.

"What did he say to you? At lunch?"

I blink, the question so foreign and strange. I feel a childish urge to refuse to answer, to withhold the information until he gives me some. I look out the window. "Very little. We're going to go on a trip to the Caribbean." My mouth curves without prompting—a quiver of excitement lighting up my body. I had the entire meal to think about it: a trip, the island sun, cold frozen drinks, nights spent in Nathan's bed, his hands on my body, mouth on my skin. I have never been out of the country, have only seen ads on television showing peaceful sunsets, steel drum music, and couples who are head over heels in love.

I snap out of my daydream, realizing that Drew has not spoken. I look up, my angle allowing me to see his profile, the tightness in his jaw alerting me that he is annoyed. The emotion baffles me. He keeps his face forward, then his jaw moves. "That's interesting."

This is the first conversation that Drew has ever instigated. My mind races. I'm searching for a question to ask him, wanting to grasp this opportunity before talkative Drew slips away. Since I married Nathan, the questions have stacked up, a teetering mountain of them in my mind. "Would you go?" The words jut out of my mouth, the question that I was too scared to ask Nathan, but one that I need the answer to.

He doesn't respond, and the silence is uncomfortable, long, and thick. "Nathan mentioned it was a business trip, and that you'd handle the arrangements. I just thought that maybe ..." I abandon the useless sentence. I shouldn't have to explain my questions; he never bothers to explain anything. He is still mad, his jaw continuing to do that clenching thing, the tension stifling in the car.

"I don't know if I am attending, but I typically don't." He flexes his hands and tightens them on the steering wheel. "When does he want to go?"

I don't know how I should feel at his words. Elated that Nathan and I will have the time alone? That is the proper response. Certainly the response that a committed, doesn't-look-at-other-men wife should have. I glance out the window, the city turning into suburbia, our Maybach catching the eye of ordinary life. I almost forget to respond, Drew's expectant silence reminding me. "Uh ... in a month. I need to get a passport."

His reflection almost hides the darkening of his eyes, the scowl across that face, the temperature in the car cooling slightly. Anger. I have no idea where it is coming from, and no idea at whom it is directed; I didn't even ask a lot of questions. I look out the window, pressing my body against the curve of the seat, wanting to put distance between me and the black cloud who is driving. Inside my mind, the questions scream for attention, their shrill shrieks causing my head to ache, building a pain in my temple that urges me to shut my eyes.

Blackness.
Road noise.
The soft sounds of music.

The headache fades, lulled to death by sleep.

I awaken in Drew's arms, his face close to mine, his arms gently lowering me into my bed. I don't think. I don't speak. I reach up, and before my mind can say a word, pull his mouth to mine.

CHAPTER 25

There is not a moment of hesitation in his kiss, his hands releasing me, his mouth following mine as I fall the final inches onto the bed. He moves above me, our lips moving, tongues intertwining, mouths crushing, tasting each other fully.

My sleep-drugged mind slowly wakes as I move, alarm bells blaring at the implications of what we are doing. But the forbiddance, the risk of being caught, only makes it hotter. My hands scramble over his chest, fumbling down to tug at his belt, my fingers frantic in their quest to have him unzipped and exposed. I can feel him pushing out, his pants tenting, his readiness impressive.

His mouth won't release mine, the scruff of his stubble burning the skin around my lips as he takes what he wants, pinning me down to the bed with his kisses. And then, finally, I have him in my hand, my palm closing around a stiff shaft. He closes his eyes and pulls away from my body.

"Wait. Take off your skirt."

I shimmy the fabric down and off, watching as he reaches into his pocket and pulls out a condom, ripping it open with his teeth, the intensity of his stare causing my breath to hitch and my mouth to water. I spread my legs before him, opening myself fully, his eyes feasting on the sight, and he kneels on the bed before me, stroking the latex of the condom down his cock.

"I know what you like," he grounds out, pressing on my opening with his stiffness. The smooth head of his latex-covered cock pushes slightly in, his face tightening when my body accepts him, my velvet lips sliding around his cock, already wet, already ready. "I've watched you fuck so many times that I feel like I've had you. Do you like when he fucks you?" He thrusts forward, my eyes closing at the sensation, a moan spilling out of my mouth. His hands flip my legs over, turning me to my side, his torso coming down, his mouth taking a greedy tour of my breast while he pumps his hips, his cock dragging slowly in and out, stretching me, the angle perfect in its sensation.

"Do you, Candy? Do you like his cock?" His words are a demand, gasping out of him, his breath haggard as he moves.

I don't answer, pulling his head down on my breasts, gasping when his mouth covers my nipple, sucking it, his eyes on me, teeth gently scraping my sensitive skin. I roll to avoid the eye contact, facing the mattress, bringing my knees beneath me and arching my back, his body moving with me, his cock beginning a faster movement, pumping in and out as his hands roam over my ass and along the line of my back.

"I've thought about this for so long," he groans. "Being inside of you. I jack off to you at night, Candy. I picture your perfect mouth sucking my cock. I think about you, just like this, bent over before me, waiting for me."

I can't respond, my mind arguing with my body that this is wrong, that I should pull off his body and walk away. But my body loves his words, loves the depth of the passion. *I* love the feeling of him inside of me, his hands now cupping my breasts, his mouth planting kisses along my back as he continues his fuck. A desperate, hurried fuck, as if he is worried that I will disappear, and he needs his fill of me first.

He is not Nathan. Our bodies do not mold in perfect synchronization, our arches and valleys do not coincide. There are times when he moves left and I move right. But he has fire for me; he cares. He is a living, breathing man who has the capacity to love, who looks at me and sees something more than a contract.

He returns me to my back, his body settling above me, his mouth softening on mine, kissing me tenderly as his strokes bring me *there*, to the point where my mind stops thinking and I come, my body clenching and contracting around him, causing his eyes to shut and, a moment later, his own finish to come.

CHAPTER 26

Life in wealth is a beautiful thing. Our streets are unclogged, our nights mosquito-free, our comfort managed and attended to twenty-four hours a day. My latest hobby is speeding, pressing the gas pedal hard enough to feel a slight vibration in my legs, my Mercedes jumping to attention, hugging the streets with a purpose. I have been pulled over twice, both times given a warning, despite my generous attempt to accept a ticket. Attempt is putting it lightly. I practically begged the officer to write me a ticket, to allow me a bad girl moment. But apparently in this county, where the streets are lined in gold and the property taxes cover more than ten times the city's budget, ticket revenue is not needed. Laws can be broken with only a slap on your diamond-studded wrist.

My tires squeal slightly as I make a too-tight, too-fast turn into the bookstore parking lot. Our corner of Nashville refuses something as tacky as a book superstore, chain stores apparently frowned upon by the uber-rich. We have no Applebees, no Gaps, no Walmarts, those storefronts replaced with organic markets, wine bars, and boutiques owned by bored housewives.

The bookstore is no different, owned by two trophy wives who had some Chardonnay one day and decided to sell books. It's housed in a three-story plantation home, different rooms dedicated to different genres, antiques and comfy couches stuffed next to towering bookshelves and stacks and piles of books. I love it.

Today I explore the *Adventure* room, located on the third floor, tall windows on one side, separated by tall bookshelves. The other side is dominated by a large map, a custom piece that shows a city-planner's view of our privileged corner of the world and the area that surrounds it.

I look at the map, my fingers trailing over the roads, finding Nathan's estate. I trace the road that leads to town, then fan out, tip-tapping across areas I haven't explored yet. Lockeland Springs. Madison. The Gulch.

"Thinking of exploring Nashville?"

I turn at the voice, one thick in a Tennessean drawl. I smile at the woman, one of the owners. She was the sort who wore diamonds with denim, and enough perfume to push me back a step. "Just realizing how little of it I've seen." I glance back at the map. "What's The Gulch?"

"Oh." She waves a hand dismissively. "You don't want to waste your time there. It's just strip clubs and head shops." She giggles, and moves closer, her long red fingernail moving across the worn paper, her next few lines lost in the hum of my mind.

"There are strip clubs here?" I interrupt her without thinking, her eyebrows raising for a moment before she responds.

"Well … yes. Of course. Hard to have a city this size without those sort of places."

"I …" I struggle for an explanation. "I just thought Tennessee didn't allow strip clubs."

She laughs off the thought, her mouth moving, more words coming out, other areas pointed out, tapas bars and parks pointed out, her nails scraping over the landscape as she rattles off a dozen things I couldn't care less about.

A wisp of something flickers in my brain, like an erratic synapse that is firing out of order, catching my attention. I reach for it, dig for it, but it is like the faded memory of a dream: gone. Street and city names float from her as my fingers move, back over the map, until my index finger comes to a slow, shuddering stop on Nathan's house.

There. I feel it again. That wisp of thought. I still, trying not to pounce too aggressively on it, trying to let it wander into the light unafraid. Unease grows in me, the thought growing legs and arms and starting a hesitant crawl through my mind. I picture Nathan, stepping into the dimly lit dump that is Sammy's. Rick's excited announcement that I was wanted in VIP. My eyes flit across his neighborhood, one that is over five hundred miles and two states, from Destin. How many strip clubs could fit into that radius? Fifty? One hundred? A hundred clubs closer than the rundown establishment that he, Drew, and Mark walked into.

So why Sammy's? And why, five minutes after stepping foot inside, did he ask for me?

CHAPTER 27

Confinement doesn't necessarily require a limited space. Confinement can be a mind fuck of restraint, a person stopped in every direction of action until they stand still in a room, afraid to move. Confinement can do strange things to a person.

Maybe that is what caused the snap. Maybe it was the two of us, both in prisons of Nathan, both desperately wanting a way out, wanting the freedom that is being withheld. I know why I am captive, my father a defenseless hour away. But what holds Drew? Why does he stay? Why does he live in this house, follow Nathan's rules, and assist in guarding my prison?

Confinement can drive a sane person mad. I have seen a chink in Drew's armor. He is human, he can stumble, and he can make mistakes. He made a mistake in touching me, in giving a drowning, lonely girl hope. Hope, and an opening.

***

I stare out the window of the limo, my legs demurely crossed, my hands clasping my clutch. I avoid looking forward to the front of the car, where I know Drew's eyes will be. Watching me. The car rides have become a source of stress for me, each moment a possible opening for Nathan to start something sexual. Tonight, at least, I am safe. We have spent all evening with Raul, a foreign investor who Nathan is courting. I don't know much except that Nathan has gone above and beyond with this man, our dinner stretching over three hours, the men already spending all day together at the site. They are drunk, their speech carrying a hint of slur, their ties loosened and spirits boisterous. Nathan sits back, and I suddenly feel his arm around my shoulders. I turn slightly to him, giving him what he wants, a loving smile, full of adoration. It is a smile I have perfected, and one he approves of.

"Did you know that Raul wanted me to find him a whore?" He enunciates the words clearly, the slur masked by his precise pronunciation. I stiffen slightly under his arm, narrowing my eyes at him as I blush appropriately, slapping his knee.

"Nathan!"

"It's true," he murmurs, bending his head to plant a soft kiss on my neck. "But I told him there is no need to waste money on a whore. Not when my wife is such an excellent fuck."

My world closes in around his words, my eyes catching his, the look in his eyes unmistakable. I beg him with my own, my mouth moving, light-hearted words coming out. "What? Nathan—stop. You're embarrassing me in front of our guest!"

We fight while smiling, his eyes demanding while mine beg. I won't do it. Fucking me in front of the staff is one thing. Offering me to a stranger something else. He tilts his head, amusement mixing with the authority in his eyes. His mouth curls, a grin stretching over it before he speaks. "Come on, honey. Show him what an amazing blow job you give."

I gasp, laughing a bit as I turn back to the window. "Next time, I'm cutting you off at the third tequila shot." I pray for solace, for him to laugh and move on, silence coming from Raul's side of the car.

"You're being rude, Candy. We've had a long night and he needs a release. Show him how an American woman can take a cock." There is an edge to his words, a warning in them, and I close my eyes at his voice.

I can't do it. I just can't. Of everything I have sold at this point in time—my dignity, my life, my past—this is one step I can't take. I feel Drew's eyes, piercing into me, pulling into my soul and judging me. I want to meet his eyes. I want to tell him that I won't do this; he doesn't need to worry. I will refuse and leave this car untainted.

Then I feel the seat shift, feel my husband's lips against my ear. "Do it, Candy. I'm not going to ask again. We have an arrangement, not a romance. Refuse and I will stop supporting your father."

My father. Nathan, in this despicable situation, brings up my father, brings his clean soul into this dirty world. Nathan knows my weakness. Knows which button to push to bring me to my knees. In this situation, literally. I turn with a coy smile, facing Raul and moving to the floor, my hands reaching out, my eyes catching Drew's and begging him to understand.

CHAPTER 28

My hand hesitates on the receiver. Making this call is a direct violation of The Agreement. The consequence: my father's well-being, the destruction of this life, however fake it is. I close my eyes and take a deep breath. He won't know. No one will ever know. I dial the number and start the call, lifting the cell phone to my ear.

"Sammy's."

Rick was always a smirker. It is something I grew to despise—that smirk. He would smirk at us when delivering bad news, smirk at patrons who had drank too much and had gotten sloppy, and smirk as his hand would travel over our bodies like we were his personal property. I can hear it through the phone, in just the one word greeting.

I grip the cell tightly, reminding myself that I am no longer Candace Tapers, the pawn of this man, dependent on him for floor placement and wages. "Hi Rick."

Silence. He's probably twisting the skin on his fat face as he tries to place the voice.

"Candy?" His tone catches me off guard, one I've never heard from him, one of fear.

I lean against the side of the gas station and hold up a finger to the high school bitch, who rolls her eyes at me. For twenty bucks, you'd think she'd be a little more accommodating.

I tuck a hand in my front pocket. "Yeah, Rick, it's me. It's been a long time." Not that long. Just over two months—but two months that have changed me in so many ways. I feel a swell of nostalgia at his voice, which is ridiculous, considering I spent the majority of my nights cursing the man's existence.

"Candy, I … it's good to hear your voice. I didn't think I'd ever hear from you again." I called him the day I signed the agreement, giving him my ten-minute notice. He hadn't asked any questions, hadn't put any of the girls on, had cut the conversation short—with a brevity that had, outlandishly enough, hurt my feelings. I hadn't expected a gold watch or a tearful response, just enough time to complete a sentence without being cut off.

"I have to ask you something. It might be hard for you to remember, but the first time Nathan came into the club—"

"I can't talk about that, Candy." His voice drops to a whisper.

"What?"

"There's nothing for me to tell you anyway. I don't know anything about them—didn't even know a name until you just said it. I didn't ask, and they didn't tell. So I can't help you."

The girl sighs, lifting her wrist and looking pointedly at her watch. I turn away from her, my shoulder digging into the brick wall. "All I want to know is if he asked for me, or if you suggested me. That first visit … when you brought me into VIP."

There is a shuffle of static and suddenly Rick's whisper is loud, as if he is cupping his hand around the receiver. "Candy, they came here *for* you. They knew everything about you before they even walked in the door."

The static ends, and there is a long stretch of silence. In it, I can almost hear my heartbeat.

"Rick?" I look at the phone, but he has hung up.

"You done?" The girl steps forward, her hand out, and I pass her the phone.

"Yeah. Thanks."

I'm done, all right. Done with whatever this shit is. I need to figure out an escape.

PART THREE

"Please. Spank me again."

CHAPTER 28

The sound of the door wakes me, the slide of glass against rubber disrupting the silence. I open my eyes, the room dim, moonlight filtering through the curtains. Then the door clicks into place, and I stiffen.

I hear the gentle slap of bare feet, and then the sink of the mattress as a figure moves across it. There is a tug on my blankets, a breeze as the fabric is lifted from my skin. Then, warmth.

He moves against my back, wrapping an arm around my waist and pulling me tightly. My body slides easily across the fine sheets, until I am solid against his. His skin is so warm, his body so hard, his arm gripping me tightly, a cocoon of embrace. I feel the scratch of stubble against my neck, and he burrows his face into my hair.

"I'm sorry."

Drew's voice is so thick, so full of emotion, one that holds and protects me. He presses a kiss against the back of my neck before continuing. "I just … I couldn't go to sleep without touching you."

I arch against him, sliding my legs between his, fitting my body even tighter into the curves of his. He reacts, his hands traveling, turning, and gripping me until there is not a single place on our bodies that doesn't connect. There is nothing for me to say—no words for what is a terrible idea. Words will only ruin this moment. Words mean thought, and I can't think about what we are doing. I know what I need. I know what I want. And right now, in this one moment, I want to be selfish.

I roll, his hands sliding and tugging to keep me close. I look into his green eyes, their depths lit with desperation. Then his gaze drops to my mouth, and I yield. He carries such a hunger for me, his desire typically locked behind a stern, rigid exterior. But here, in the privacy of my bedroom, with Nathan's room a stone's throw away, he releases it; a storm of want, his passion breathtaking in its simplicity. He follows his line of sight, lowering his mouth to mine, his hands pulling my waist, a strong leg wrapping around me and drawing me close.

Kissing him is so different than Nathan. Nathan and I have emotional expression in our kisses, our lips able to communicate in ways that we will never verbalize. Drew's eyes, his touch, his words— they tell me everything I need to know. His kiss is more of a sexual fire, taking this sweet, needy moment and pouring the kerosene of passion onto it. It starts off slow, our movements still drugged with sleep. Soon, it flares, his hands moving quicker, pulling me upright, yanking at the silk of my camisole until it's over my head and I'm half naked before him. He moves to his knees, our kisses frantic, our hands twisting into each other's hair, tugging and pulling. Then I am pushed back and I feel the slide of cotton against skin as my boyshorts take the long journey down my legs and off my body.

He kneels on the bed between my legs, my body naked before him. He pulls up my legs, placing my feet on his bare chest, his hands running softly along my legs, a look of drugged arousal heavy in his eyes. And there before me, lit by the moonlight, I can't help but compare them.

He is rugged where Nathan is finely cut, scruffy where Nathan is smooth. They have the same messy hair—hair that is short enough to be professional but long enough to grip in my hand and pull. His chest is covered in a thin layer of dark hair where Nathan's is smooth, his abs thicker where Nathan's are thinner, his build stronger, evidencing his strength.

I love the look of my feet on his chest; I love the contrast of my lighter skin against his darker, delicate feet against masculine strength. He leans slightly forward, digging my feet into his pectoral muscles and his hands slide down the inside of my legs, pressing gently out as he moves, my feet sliding off his chest, my breath hitching as my legs fully open. His hand gently touches the smooth skin in between them.

"Drew, I …" I stop talking, his fingers sliding along my wet slit, his eyes on mine. Then he lowers his head, moving his hands to my thighs, and his eyes are on nothing but me. My face burns, and I prop myself up, about to protest, my mouth forming the words. Then I see him and stop, my mouth dropping open slightly, the view so carnal I almost moan.

He is examining me, his fingers sliding down my thighs and massaging the skin on either side of my pussy, opening and closing the lips, his warm breath tickling the skin, making every movement of my skin tickle in the most tantalizing way.

He glances up, his eyes black with need. "God, I needed this," he groans, lowering his hot mouth onto me, my back arching at the shock of his hot, wet mouth, the soft trail of his tongue as it flickers lightly over my clit, his entire mouth working in perfect coordination to bring all of my senses to that spot.

My back hits the sheets, my hands reaching out and fisting fabric, the surrender of my body to him complete, his face buried in my most private place, doing something that is too perfect, his tongue knowing—without instruction—just how gently to sweep over my clit, just how to draw me into his mouth, how to use his entire mouth and not just his tongue. That look on his face, before he buries his mouth on me, is one a recovering alcoholic gives an ice-cold beer. Ravenous need. And it is obvious, from the sounds and expertise that he is showing below, that he loves what he is doing. It is something that I will do with him whenever—holy shit. I am about to come, my back arching, the swell of pleasure interrupting my thought processes, interrupting everything within a half mile radius, so pure and intense, swelling up the hill, small whimpers coming from me as it climbs.

Then, pure silence, my body wracking beneath his mouth, his tongue maintaining the perfect flutter against my small bud of nerves until my breaking point—a point he somehow instinctively knows. As I fall down that hill of pleasure, his tongue gently carries me down, slowly, softening imperceptibly, until I sink into a sea of perfect, post-coital bliss, my world going dark, every sense leaving my body in one perfect moment.

Jello has nothing on my limbs, their loose and pliable movement easily manipulated by his hands. He moves my legs, lifts my torso, and tucks my body underneath the sheets, pulling the soft weight of a down comforter over me. I murmur words of nonsense, trying to follow his movement, his soft chuckle irritating me briefly, my heavy eyes uncooperative. A sigh of relief leaves me when I feel the blanket lift, feel his heat settle in behind me, his arms stealing around my body, his lips gently touching my neck. "Sleep," he whispers.

I should be offering to take care of him. I should be rolling over, pushing him to his back and dragging those way-too-sexy sweatpants off his hard, muscular hips. But I don't. I grip his arm tightly across my chest and close my eyes, the relaxation of release bringing sleep to me quickly.

I don't wake when he leaves my bed, returning to the big glass house and his portion of it. I don't notice when my alarm sounds; I sleep right through my morning routine and—for the first time in five weeks—don't dress in case Nathan calls.

I open my eyes to the unfamiliar view of full sunshine against the vaulted rafters. I have not prepared for him, an oversight that went unnoticed; Nathan's morning schedule one that didn't include me. And I wonder, lazily, if this is the beginning of my end.

CHAPTER 30

I feel like I am a cocktail of sorts, different mixers and alcohol being added, the flavor and consistency changing with each new addition.

I can feel a break coming, my psyche sick of the rollercoaster of emotions it is riding. I can only harness rebellion and self-esteem for so long before my mind is going to say *fuck you* and kill everyone in the room. It's only taken five weeks for me to realize I can't be Anna Nicole Smith, unless Anna Nicole was a dominatrix who told the old man what the fuck to do. I am not good at being meek and mild and shutting my mouth. I can feel my body itching, feel my mind pushing against the restraints, testing for weak areas, searching for hidden passageways and loopholes to freedom.

But I can't escape, can't run, can't ask Nathan for a divorce. First, I need to figure out what to do with my father.

His health seems to be in a limbo of sorts. He is healing, his color returning, his medication not as life-sustaining as it originally was. But his improvement is at a slow pace and is unpredictable in its path. One day he is smiling, the next week I am met by Pam with sober eyes and a tight mouth, his health taking a hard right turn into serious. The problem child was first his immune system, then his kidneys. His vulnerable spots seem to change, having no rhyme or reason in their locations or symptoms. Today is a bad day, in the middle of a bad week. His breath is labored, and he has been unresponsive all day. His drugs are at a level that keep him one step above comatose, his sleep heavy, his hand limp when I pick it up.

The responsibility for his care weighs heavily on me, slowing down and tripping normal brain functions. I should be able to figure this out. I should be able to have a clear, concise thought process and come up with a plan.

The truth of the matter is, I can avoid any heavy lifting of my brain. The correct path is smooth and well-marked.

Separate myself from Drew.
Follow the rules.
Stop asking questions.
Visit my father and support him in every way possible.

I can live my golden life, squash the ridiculous theories that my mind has been concocting, and listen to Nathan. Ride his cock, obey his rules, and deal with the minor items that separate this life and Happily Ever After. That is the unselfish choice, one that will guarantee my father the level of care that he needs.

I don't feel the tears. They slide down my cheeks, salt paths through expensive foundation. I don't realize it until I feel a soft hand on my shoulder and look up into Pam's concerned face. She offers me a tissue, crouching beside me before wrapping her arms around my neck. The kind gesture breaks a dam of some sort, and a sob slips out, my own hands reaching around to return the hug. "It's okay, Mrs. Dumont," she whispers. "I promise, he'll get over this little bump."

I shake my head against the stiff curls of her hair. "Oh, Pam. It's so much more than that."

CHAPTER 31

I believe, with all of the rules involved in my life, my heart should have some. It shouldn't be allowed to care for a man who is incapable of loving it back. It shouldn't be allowed to care for a man who puts my father's well-being at risk. And it shouldn't fall for more than one man at one time.

My heart, like the rest of my body, doesn't like to follow rules.

I have no reason to care for Nathan. Outside of sex, he is cold and distant—a dictator who has constructed this world of hateful rules. It is the glimpses that have done me in. Nathan in Napa, his soft words, loving glances, thoughtful gestures and carefree smile. The glimpses of compassion when he asks about my father, or the rare moments when I catch him in a genuine smile. Those glimpses have hacked the walls I've built between us to bits.

And if those bits are kindling, our sex is the blowtorch, held just above their sticks. Our long, hot fucks that have occurred in every part of the house, no matter who is around, or *because* of who is around—the raw need which he displays, the fever that burns in his eyes, the possession of his gorgeous face—every session is a new study in addicts who cannot get enough of each other. I am at the point of needing his body, craving its domination, the slick slide of his cock in and out, the delicious terse growl of demands.

I don't understand why Nathan is so cold, why he doesn't let me stay in his bed. Has he ever been in a relationship? Has he ever been the happy, carefree man he so convincingly portrays in public?

I used to ask Drew those questions, though he'd never respond. Now, due to our affair, I have no one to ask.

Affair. It sounds so dirty. *I am a cheating wife.* I recognize the truth in the statement, but still attempt to justify this twisted triangle, if it can be considered one. The three points of us are all so badly contorted; our emotions and lives too gnarled to have something so simple as points.

I think of Drew, in his lonely corner of the triangle, and feel such confusion. The whispered words of Rick play in my mind. "They knew everything about you." *They.* Drew included. He has been involved since the beginning. He is the one, when I tried to decide whether to sign my life away, urged me forward, spelling out my pathetic life and dire financial situation.

I have slept with the man, yet he has never shared why I am here, why they walked into Sammy's and asked for me. He has never answered my questions, hinted into my situation, or looked the other way so that I could bend a rule. He is my jailor as much as Nathan.

He seems entitled to sample from my body—but, unlike Nathan, he offers nothing in return.

CHAPTER 32

Nathan has spent the day at home, working in his office. I've watched him through the windows, disguising my snooping behind a swim, then a few hours poolside with a book. Two men came at noon, going over documents with him and then leaving, Nathan returning to his seat, his hands running through his hair, frustration marring that beautiful face.

I feel like a voyeur, watching him from behind my sunglasses, marveling at how I still find him sexy, his loosened tie and rolled up sleeves, the darkness on his face when he barks into the phone.

I am getting turned on, a ridiculous side effect of boredom and Nathan's presence, and I set down the book, stretching my arms upward, in the most attention-seeking move I have. I coil my hair into a knot and wander toward the edge of the pool, taking a long moment to adjust my bikini bottoms before I dive into the pool.

He is a sickness. I decide that on lap twelve. A virus that I cannot combat. Despite his incredible talent at being an asshole, I want his touch, want his approval. I want a cure but fear I would hesitate to take the medication.

I come up for air and he is there, standing at the edge of the pool, his hands on his hips. "Get out."

I duck underneath and smile, swimming toward the edge and pushing up and over the side. My exit is less than graceful, my sexpot moment passing, but I manage to stand, water running off of me and staining the pavers underneath my feet. His eyes take in my bikini, the thin cords that run to small triangles, my breasts practically bare before him. He steps closer, his eyes flicking upward and meeting mine.

We stare at each other, our connection unwavering as he lowers both hands to my breasts, sliding his palms under the wet fabric and squeezing. My eyes close slightly, pleasure sweeping through me, and he rubs rough thumbs over my nipples. "Open your eyes. Look at me."

I respond, opening my eyes and looking up, his blue depths studying me, noting the hitch in my breath when he squeezes, the slight drop of my bottom lip as need grows.

"I've been working," he says roughly. "*Trying* to work. Do you have any idea how hard I get when I see your body?"

He waits for a response, my mouth moving without sound. I clear my throat, almost whispering the words. "No sir."

"Feel it. Now."

My hands move quickly, jumping into to action, anxious for what awaits them. Wet hands on expensive fabric, unzipping and unbuttoning, reaching in and grabbing impressive, hard heat. Rock hard. *Ready.*

He bats my hands away, pulling at the strings of my top and letting it fall on the pool deck, the sun hitting my swollen breasts, the nipples hard and aching from his touch, then steps back, looking my body up and down. "Go in my office and get on your knees. You're going to finish what you started."

I move quickly, his presence behind me, my skin tightening as I move into the air-conditioned house. My feet cover the distance, turning corners and then stepping onto the plush rug of his office, my damp feet sinking into its mat.

"Before the chair. Kneel."

His order comes from behind me, and I do as I am told, my knees hitting the floor, his steps coming beside me, my eyes looking up to find him staring down at me.

"Perfect," he said hoarsely, sitting down and reaching in his pants, pulling out his cock and laying it out before me. "Swallow it. Deep."

He keeps his eyes on me, watching as I run my hands over its length, wetting my lips and inching closer, trying to keep my eyes on his but pulled to the magnificent sight before me. It twitches beneath my hands, and he pulls on the back of my head, eager to have it in my mouth.

When I close my mouth on it, sliding my lips over his head, the veins in his cock swollen under my fingers, he groans. A long, slow groan of release, satisfaction. He cradles my hair in his hands, his head tilted, watching me suck, watching my eyes close as I gag, the width and depth of him too great to take.

"Fuck," he swears. "Do you know how often I think about you at work? Think about you just like this, behind my desk? I get fucking hard thinking about you." He pushes my head harder, sitting up slightly and watching the slide of his cock intently.

His cell buzzes, on the desk, and he reaches for it, his eyes never leaving mine. He answers the phone, pulling at my head, his eyes ordering me to continue.

"Hello." He almost growls the word, inhaling sharply when I suck a little harder. I love the taste of his skin. How hard he grows in my mouth, the moments when I taste the sweet drops of his arousal. There is nothing that turns me on more than having him before me, his hands urging me on, his most sensitive organ twitching underneath my tongue. I work my hand over his length, pulling him from my mouth and moving below, taking his balls into my mouth, and rolling them along my tongue, his words pausing in their speech, a brief hitch in his tone.

I smile, skimming my teeth lightly over the skin, watching his eyes close briefly, his voice struggle to return to the conversation, his words halting when they come. I return to his cock, sucking with renewed energy, my hands and my mouth working in a wet, sexual tandem.

He stands, pulling my head back slowly, dark eyes watching as inch after inch of his cock leaves my mouth, my cheeks hollowing from the suction, my tongue teasing and flicking as he pulls me off. "John. My wife needs me. I'll call you back." He ends the call and tosses the phone aside, pulling me to my feet in one quick movement.

"Bend over. In my chair. Right fucking now."

He yanks at the strings of my bikini bottom, pulling it away before I am in place, my knees hitting his chair a moment later. It is a wide leather chair, worn and sitting low, my knees putting me at the perfect height for his entrance. He pushes a finger inside, swearing when he feels my readiness. "Is that from this?" he asks, thrusting inside, my insides tightening around him, anxious for every inch of his entry. "Does it turn you on to suck my cock?"

I nod, knowing that it won't be enough. Knowing that he will want more, will want to hear my voice. But I want the reaction my silence will bring. He slaps my ass, the hard, rough impact against my skin causing me to jump, to moan, the possessiveness of the contact causing a curl of pleasure to shoot through my body. "Answer me."

"Yes." I gasp. "Please. Spank me again."

He waits, fucking me hard, the percussion of our skin quick, the anticipation of his touch causing my legs to tighten, my core to grip him tightly. It is building, my mountain of lust, my body shaking and breaking around his stiff rod, each thrust perfectly timed, the entire act too erotic for me to take. Being fucked like a whore, I am learning, turns me the fuck on. Then it comes, another open hand slap against my skin, his fingers gripping after each contact is made, each stinging stroke taking me closer and closer until

Ecstasy.

My body breaks into a thousand splinters of pleasure, a series of gasps spilling out, my back arching and pushing against his hard pelvis, our bodies joined as I am torn apart in a sea of desire.

CHAPTER 33

If this woman paid money for these lips, she needs a refund. I pick up a spinach stuffed croissant and take a tiny bite, watching the blonde's giant lips wrap around the edge of a wine glass. I laugh at a joke another woman says, and wish for some hard liquor.

It's amazing how similar a wine charity luncheon can be to stripping. In both, I fake interest, laughing at bad jokes, smiling at conversations I couldn't care less about. In both, I give compliments I don't mean, and fake emotions I don't feel. In both, I'm judged, though it's funny—in stripping, I was judged for my body. Here, I am judged because of it. Not that they are that obvious. Oh no, they act sweet, but I see the daggers in their glances, the fangs in their smiles. At least in stripping, the assholes are upfront about it. Here, I have to learn an entirely different game to play, the current one against ... I silently count my opponents, my eyes hopping across the expensively attired women perched around Nathan's living room, their hands filled with Beth's finger foods, most sinking comfortably into their second wine glass. Ten women.

Of all of Nathan's demands, this has been one of the hardest to take. I had balked when he brought it up, my lonely boredom not to the stifling degree that I wanted to entertain strangers.

"You're doing it." Three words tersely delivered over his morning eggs, his fork scraping the plate as he scooped up his final bite and stood, lifting his coffee cup for a quick sip. "The battered women's shelter is a good cause, and one of my sister's passions. It'll be good for you to get involved." *His sister.* It was his first mention of her, though I've seen her photo around the house, and Mark mentioned that she passed away a couple of years ago.

So here I am, hosting a two hour "meeting" that has skipped over a variety of topics, none of which seemed to concern battered women and most of which has centered on gossip. I pick at my plate and daydream about our Bahamas trip, now only one week away, assuming my new passport arrives in time. I'm ready for it, my excitement building with each passing day, despite my best attempts at setting low expectations.

"So, Janice." A leggy brunette with boobs as big as my head, leans forward; and it takes a moment to realize she is talking to me.

"It's Candace." I correct her, and when she smiles, I can see a wedge of spinach in her teeth.

"Right." She brushes off my name with a flick of her diamond studded hand. I run a thumb over my ring, a simple three carat princess cut diamond that—in any other scenario—I would have swooned over. But in this life, it feels like a shackle. Did hers feel the same way? How many of these women, each pampered and glistening with the sparkle of upper class wealth—how many of them hate their lives? My gaze drifts back to the woman, who has her brow raised in the expectant manner of someone who is waiting on a response.

"I'm sorry?" I start to cross my legs, then stop, pinning my knees together.

"I asked if you ever knew *Cecile*." There is a gleam in her eyes, one that raises an alarm and reminds me that I am a spindly gazelle, surrounded by a pride of lions.

"Cecile?" I glance at the other women, to see if anyone else is listening to this conversation. They are. All of them, their bodies tilted forward in the subtle manner of eavesdroppers everywhere. Whoever Cecile is, I'm suddenly as interested in her as they appear to be.

"Why yes." The brunette smiles in a smug manner that makes me vow, right then, to not tell her about the spinach, which has now shifted to a front row location that is hysterically apparent. "Nathan's fiancée."

My stomach flips at the title. I've wondered a lot of things about

Nathan, including his past dating history. Was this fiancée a contract girl, like me, one that backed out of the deal? Or was she legitimate, someone he loved, and who loved him in return? I feel a stab of jealousy at the latter option, and glance down before the emotion shows in my face.

Whatever she has to say, I'm not sure I want to hear it. I reach forward, piercing a crab cake ball with a toothpick and pop it into my mouth. I chew, turning toward the curly-headed bean stalk to my right, and search for something to say.

"Hasn't he told you what happened?" She doesn't give up, all but waving her hands at me in an attempt to draw attention to the question.

I swallow, and try to ignore her, my hands flexing on my thighs, an exhale hissing through my lips. I try. I fail. I turn back to her, my voice as calm as I can manage it.

"What happened?"

"Well that's just the thing." She leans forward as if her next sentence might change my world. "No one knows. One week, they were planning their reception and sampling wedding cake. The next week, she just *disappeared*."

She disappeared? I think of my past life, and the sudden exit, no explanations given, my stuff packed up by strangers. I disappeared, and yet here I am, perfectly fine, save my junk food deprivation. Maybe Cecile's the same way. Maybe a sexy man waltzed into her life, offered her the moon, and she took it.

I discard the idea as soon as it hits. What man could compete with Nathan? Especially if this bitch had been getting Napa Valley Nathan. There is no amount of money, or sex appeal, that could compete with that Nathan.

But if not that ... then what?

I glance at my watch and wish these women would hurry this meeting the hell up. If Nathan's fiancée disappeared, that only makes my next step that much more important.

***

They finally stand, hugs and air kisses all around, promising to get together soon, flowery bullshit stacked upon flowery bullshit. It's been, in terms of the women's shelter, a complete waste of two and a half hours. I sit in the window seat, watching them walk down the front steps, and will them to hurry-the-fuck-up, to get into their cars and off of this property, so that I will be alone with Drew. Today is a quiet day—no Beth, no landscapers, no housekeepers. It will be just him and me, and I plan to take full advantage of the opportunity. Not just to seduce, but in hopes of getting access to the house, my fingers itching to explore Nathan's office and what he may hide there.

Drew walks in, glancing out the front windows. "Why are you still in here?"

I keep the smile on my face. "Nathan is always so concerned with appearances. I thought it'd be odd for me to run to the guest house before they pull out."

He nods, and turns away. "I'm sorry for coming into your room the other night." His words are soft, almost whispered, even though the cameras are off—the security system only activated at night and by his control.

I say nothing, swallowing, and look out the front window, seeing the cars stop at our gate, the wrought iron slowly opening. *He's sorry.* He certainly should be. He's put me in a terrible position, he's put my agreement with Nathan in jeopardy, and risked my father's health in doing so. But this sudden change of conscience is terrible in its timing.

The cars in the driveway move, passing through the gates and out of sight. I wait until the last one pulls through, then stand. Moving to him, I look up into his face, pulling his face down and forcing him to look at me. "Drew, please stop talking."

I can feel his reluctance in every move, his eyes slowly dragging to mine, his body stiff against mine. He pushes away, a hurried gesture, hard on my shoulders, and steps back. "No."

My heart sinks, my plan thwarted.

"Not here. It's too visible." He strides toward the back hall, grabbing my hand and pulling me along with him.

We enter his room, my introduction a blur of cream walls and masculine furniture, any observations lost in the moment that he pulls me onto his bed. Sex the first time was hurried, him demanding permission with his body, my own response hesitant, terrified of the giant cliff that we were taking a step off of. This time I hold nothing back, letting his hunger devour me, his hands placing my body where and how he wants it. And this time, he's the one who seems unsure of the wisdom of our actions.

He pushes me against the wall, his hands fumbling with my shorts, jerking them down so he can lift and wrap my legs around his body. He whispers words that contradict his motions. "Are you sure? We shouldn't…" Then he groans as my legs pull him tight, his body supporting me against the wall, my arms wrapping around his neck and pulling his mouth to mine. I yank at his shirt while we kiss, pulling the fabric up, our mouths separating for a brief moment as it pulls over his head. His hands move beneath me, unzipping, yanking, ripping open a condom, an initial bump of bare cock against the curve of my skin, then it is covered.

Thrusts. Our bodies on the bed, my legs spread before him, his hips moving in strong, slow fucks that are increasing in rhythm. It is a beautiful sight, the daylight showing me all of the details my dim bedroom hid—his eyes blazing with possession, his chest tightening, the slide of his cock as it thrust, his gaze dropping to watch it, his mouth slightly open in lust. He grips my thighs, holding my legs against his chest, and he releases any control, starting a furious pace that has my body shaking, intensity building.

Orgasms. Mine while he is behind me, his balls drilling a steady beat on my clit, his hands squeezing my ass, holding me still while he sets the pace, bringing me to completion. His while I am beneath him, his arms framing my head while he thrusts inside of me, his mouth brushing mine, the pace increasing until he grunts, shudders, and then whispers my name, lowering his body to mine, giving one final full thrust that takes him completely inside of me.

***

I hear the rush of water as he opens his shower door and steps in. I sit up, moving quickly and silently off his bed and out to the hall. To be safe, I am giving myself four minutes, my feet running as soon as my bare soles touch the cool tile. I trace the path Drew led me down one week earlier, the path to Nathan's office.

I skid around the edge of his desk, my hand gripping the wooden edge, tugging on handles and drawer pulls until one slides open. Files. There has to be *something* on me, a folder of my history, or a diagram of their evil plan. I skim the folder titles.

Three minutes.

The drawer seems to be filled with mostly family-related items.

Dumont Family History.
Dumont Estate.
Dumont Trust.
Files for names I am not familiar with, most likely his parents. I see my name, and time slows.

CANDACE

The title is written as painstakingly neat as the rest of the tabs, my place equal among his family files. I almost missed the file, its thin depth lying against the one before it, shielded by a tag with similar placement. I reach forward and pull it out.

Two minutes.

My heart sinks as the file slides out quickly and easily, its weight too light to hold many secrets. It feels, in fact, empty. I open it slowly, and my eyes fall on a single piece of paper. It is a piece of Nathan's letterhead, a half-page card that is familiar enough to my eyes, the embossed letters of his name across the top. On it, in the painstakingly neat writing of my husband, is one short message. I read it quickly, then stop, my heart thudding heavily in my chest— slow, loud thumps that rattle my thinking. I read it again.

I loved Candace more than I have ever loved another soul on this planet. Her death leaves a hole in my heart that will never be filled. Please respect our privacy in this difficult time.

One minute.

CHAPTER 34

I am back in Drew's bed when he emerges, his hair wet, a towel around his shoulders, his jeans unbuttoned and hanging low on firm, muscular hips. I stretch, my body still naked, in hopes of distracting him from any erratic thoughts. The shower had been off when I returned, no rush of water to hide the sound of the door. I close my eyes, trying to keep my face smooth and calm, trying to paint the picture of a woman whose heart is not racing, whose mind is not panicking.

"We can't keep doing this. I can't ..." His words hang, unfinished, and I open my eyes to see him bend down, picking up his shirt and walking to the edge of my bed, his eyes traveling over my skin until they stop at my face. He puts a knee on the bed, leaning over to brush his lips over my skin, placing soft kisses on my stomach, the underside of my breast, my collarbone, and then my lips. He studies me, his green eyes cloudy. "Neither one of us deserves you," he says, standing up and buttoning his pants.

I roll over, facing the opposite direction, and hug his pillow.

I loved Candace more than I have ever loved another soul on this planet.

Loved me? A lie, like every photo taken by the press, like that entire weekend at Napa Valley.

Her death leaves a hole in my heart that will never be filled.

There are very few explanations for that line, written on Nathan's stationary, in handwriting I recognize as his, placed in a folder that bears my name. My mind can only grasp one. In Nathan's world—his meticulously scheduled, perfectly planned universe—I'm going to die.

It's planned for, a statement already prepared, everything in place except for my dead body. When? And why?

"You need to go back."

I nod, rolling off the bed and standing, accepting the clothes that he hands over. I don't bother dressing, giving him a tight smile and leaving, walking naked through the house and back to the guesthouse, glancing at the clock as I crawl into the bed. Five hours until Nathan arrives home. Five hours before the next man fucks with my mind.

Please respect our privacy in this difficult time.

Cecile disappeared. I can't. I can't run away from Nathan, not without something in place for my father's care. No matter the reason, no matter how unhappy I am as his wife, or whatever danger might exist, I am now in the rare position of being able to actually help my father. To provide for him, visit with him, financially support his care—not just through this sickness, but for the rest of his life.

I can't just toss this opportunity away.

***

"What happens to my father upon my death?" I finger the ripped buttons of a Chanel blouse, one I took the tags off this morning, wondering if it is salvageable. Nathan had ripped it open without concern for the fine fabric, his need too great for something as silly as unbuttoning.

Nathan's head snaps up so quickly that I hear a bone pop. "What do you mean?"

I drop the shirt and reach for my skirt, stepping into it sans underwear, not wanting to hunt for them in the sheets of Nathan's bed. "I mean, if I die, what happens to my father? Would you continue to provide for his care?" *I shouldn't have said anything.* One of the unwritten rules, made clear by Nathan's attitude, is that I get up and leave after sex. No chitchat, no goodbye kiss, just a quick and silent exit.

"Do you *plan* on dying?" His face is almost distraught, his question spoken quickly and urgently. My suicide must clash with his current plans.

"No. I don't think anyone *plans* on dying. But what would happen if I do? The agreement doesn't mention anything about that." An omission which leads me to think that my father will be left high and dry upon my expiration.

He frowns. "I can have my attorney draft an amendment. I guess I didn't expect your father to outlive you." His blue eyes lock with mine, a silent appraisal in them.

"I would like that," I say quietly, zipping up the side of my skirt.

He fastened the buttons of one sleeve, his expression grave. "Then I'll do it this week."

This week. I can see the thoughts growing, his mind working through my questions. I ball up the broken shirt in my hand and scoop up my heels, leaving the room and heading outside, putting distance between us before he starts asking questions of his own.

NATHAN

He watches her leave, her posture strong, despite all he's put her through. He watches her pull at the glass slider, the moonlight softening the lines of her face, then she is gone. She's left a dozen times, and never has the urge been so strong to ask her to stay. Only this time, it isn't his heart that tempts the action—it's his head.

He picks up his phone, dialing Drew's cell, the man quickly answering.

"Turn on the security system. Then come here." He ends the call and stands at the window, watching her pull the curtains of her home closed, the cream drapes glowing as she turns on the interior lights.

"What's up?" The man steps in, his law enforcement bearing present, even in gym shorts and a T-shirt.

"We have a problem. It's Candy." He sighs, telling the man of her questions and watching his face pinch in worry. "I'm worried … with her references to dying … Maybe I've gone too far in trying to keep her at arm's length."

"I wouldn't call anything about your relationship 'arm's length'." The response is sharper than it needs to be, and Nathan lifts his gaze to the man's.

"What's your point?"

"I just don't want you to forget the goal of all this."

"We leave for the Bahamas next week. You don't have to worry about me *forgetting* anything."

"Not the money. *Her.*" An outsider would think they are talking about Candy, but he knows who Drew is talking about, hears the

165

protective growl in his voice, sees the tightening of his jaw.

"I don't owe Cecile any loyalty. Not after all this time."

Drew scowls. "And what about Candy? You even care if she's suicidal?"

"Of course I care." Nathan crosses his arms over his chest. "Don't challenge me in one breath about developing feelings for her, and the next about not giving a shit. You're talking out of both sides of your mouth, and all of it's bullshit considering the way you've been eye fucking her."

"There's nothing in her contract about loyalty." Drew smirks, and Nathan takes a step forward, dropping his hands, and fighting the urge to tighten them into fists.

"But there is something in yours." He tilts his head, watching the man's face, the pit in his stomach turning into a sharp pain. "Tell me you haven't touched her."

In the silence, a piece of him, one recently created, dies. He steps closer. "Tell me that you haven't touched *my wife*."

"Your wife?" The man laughs, and it is a steel blade in between his ribs. "You're not in love with her," Drew spits out. "You're in love with Cecile. Candy is a fucking contract. Nothing more."

"I'll decide what Candy is."

"No." Drew shakes his head. "She's not a fucking building, Nathan. She'll decide what she is."

He fights the urge to punch him, to smash bones and bloody knuckles. But there's a reason, other than Cecile, that he keeps the man around. The handgun tucked in his waistband. The ability of the man to take a life with his bare hands. Still, Nathan's temper rages, and he forces out the next question through clenched teeth. "Have. You. *Touched.* Her?"

"Yes." The response is a challenge, and Nathan steps forward, so close that they are eye to eye. He shouldn't care. Their marriage is a business arrangement. It wasn't designed for love or emotions, and he'd gone out of his way to make sure she didn't develop any. He shouldn't care, but he does. Inside, somewhere past the anger with Cecile, the hurt of his heart, the plans that they've made … he cares.

The punch comes from another man, one without structure or control, a man he thought he buried a long time ago. It hits Drew's jaw and the pain radiates through his fist, the crunch and impact of bones and flesh brutal in its ferocity. There is the silent collision of his bare chest against Drew's shirt, muscles struggling for control. They hit the wall and a Peter Lik print shudders. Drew's hand moves and Nathan freezes in the cock of his gun.

"What are you doing?" Drew steps back, both hands wrapped around the gun, his stance born from years of training. "Are you *fucking* kidding me right now?

"Do you love her?" Nathan hisses out the question, his shoulders slumping against the wall as he lifts this hands and rests them on his head.

"Not yet." Drew moves a step to the right, the position probably better for taking a man's life.

"Then stop. Everything. I'll need you this week, but when we leave for Nassau, you pack your shit and get the fuck out."

The man scowls. "So, that's it. Fuck Cecile or anything else. You go to Nassau, execute your plan, and then wash your hands of me? And what if you get caught?"

"I'm not going to get caught." Not with Candace.

"If you do, I'm not involved. I'm not covering for you, and I'm not cleaning up your mess."

"Your sister got me into this fucking mess. Let's not forget that." It's not a fair thing to say. Fuck, the whole situation is unfair. Maybe it's wrong to fire him. But the man shouldn't have put his hands on his wife. Nathan closes his eyes, assaulted by the thought of her body moving underneath Drew's, her lips wrapping around his cock. He jerks to his feet and almost lunges for the man again, regardless of the gun in his hand.

Drew straightens, his gun falling, and clears the bullet from the chamber. There is the tinny sound of metal against tile as the bullet drops to the floor, rolling harmlessly away. "Are we done with this shit?"

Nathan crosses his arms. "We're done."

"I'll be out of here by the time you're back from your trip." He tips an imaginary hat at Nathan and steps back. "Enjoy your wife. I certainly did."

The rage explodes in his chest, and it takes everything in him to not chase the man down the hall and kill him.

Four years since Cecile, four years that had built a friendship between the two of them, one that—two months ago—seemed ironclad.

He turns and walks to the window, looking at the guesthouse, her lights still on.

She isn't worth it. Not with everything currently at stake.

CHAPTER 35

I can't sleep, my mind running laps, my conversation with Nathan only raising more questions. Thinking about my situation seems to do nothing but stress me the hell out. I kick off the covers and stand, my muscles jumping, my head aching with the effort of trying to not think. Swimming. Maybe that will clear my head, exhaust my muscles, and allow my body to finally sleep. I step to the curtains and slip through, unlocking the slider and stepping outside.

It is beautiful on this ledge of the world. The house sits on the edge of a stiff drop, looking down on the city below. It is a city that sleeps with lights on, skyscrapers announcing their greatness with uplights and a blatant waste of electricity, dotting the landscape with colorful dots all hours of the night. I turn to the house, following the simple, modern lines of the architecture, the house designed to make an impression, from the front as well as the back, the floor to ceiling windows disappearing into the night sky. As I watch, the house goes dark, the light in Nathan's room turning off.

I wonder where Drew is, and whether he came for me tonight. Earlier, I put a note on the glass. On it, I wrote only 'No.' I figured that would be clear enough for him, yet cryptic enough that—if seen by someone else's eyes—wouldn't rat out our affair. I'm not ready to see Drew. Not ready to accept the fact that he may be involved in a plot to cause me harm.

I pull my t-shirt over my head and slide my pajama pants off, leaving them both in a pile on the pool deck, standing naked on the edge of the pool. I stare into the ripples of water, the lights constantly changing the color of the water, making the transition from cool to warm, from icy to red-hot. I dive when it is the color of blood, needing to see the color change while underwater, needing to feel transformed, from blood red to relaxation blue. When blue steals over the space, I close my eyes and start my laps.

I have memorized this pool, every inch of it, my mind and body knowing exactly how many strokes, how many kicks, how many breaths to take before I reach the edge. I swim, then tuck, roll, push, and return the opposite direction. Back.
Forth.
Back.
Forth.

Twenty laps. Thirty laps. Forty laps. I try for fifty, my legs giving out at lap forty-two, my chest aching, arms shaking, strokes slowing until I stop, in the middle of the pool, in the middle of the lap. I roll over and float on my back, keeping my eyes closed, my chest heaving as I fight to slow my gasps.

When I finally open my eyes, it is to an orchestra of stars—thousands of identical specks. Under them, on my back, I feel so small. Small and tired, my eyes heavy. I right my body, my feet standing, moving sluggishly through the thick water to the steps, my gait quickening as I leave the weight of the water and enter the heat of the night. I ignore my clothes and pull on the slider, shivering slightly when I step into the cool room, my weary arms pulling the door closed and locking it.

I wrap a towel around my body, and crawl into bed, pulling the comforter over my body and closing my eyes. And finally, without argument, my mind goes to sleep.

***

Something is wrong. The first sign came this morning, when Nathan called my room personally and asked me to come to the house. *Asked.* Physically said the words, 'Will you come to the house?' I don't think the words 'Will you' have ever left that gorgeous mouth of his.

When I walked in, prepared for his hands, his mouth, his cock, Drew and Nathan stood in the kitchen, their eyes on me, watching me closely. An arrangement of flowers sat between them, roses and lilies spilling out of an arrangement that stood four feet high. I walked carefully toward them, my eyes flicking back and forth, trying to read the serious look on their faces.

"These are for you," Nathan said stiffly, stepping to the side and gesturing to the flowers.

I looked at them in confusion, staying in place. "Are we expecting guests?"

Nathan flinched. "No. I ordered them for you. You like flowers, right?"

"Yes…" I stare at the flowers, trying to figure out what is going on. "Why?"

"Is it not big enough?" The tightness in Nathan's voice causes me to turn, my eyes noting several details at once. His tight grip on the bar stool before him. The intense contact of his blue eyes. The way his polo hugs the muscles of his chest tightly, emphasizing the cut of his build.

I step forward, approaching the arrangement with trepidation.

"The flowers are fine. What is their purpose?"

"I can't be nice?" he asks shortly.

I glance from him to Drew, and if the tension in the room was any thicker, we'd all suffocate. I try to laugh, the sound coming out wrong. "Did I do something wrong?" He knows about Drew. He must have found out about Drew.

He steps forward. "How unhappy are you?" He grips my wrists and pulls, turning me to face him. "Are you unhappy?"

I bristle, yanking my arm away and stepping toward the door. "Does it *matter*? I wasn't aware that anyone cared about my personal happiness."

"It matters if you are planning on killing yourself."

His voice is so quiet, so deadly serious, that I pause in my exit, turning to face him. He stares at me, his face grim.

"Killing myself?" The thought is so absurd that, this time, a genuine laugh comes out. "Why would I do *that*? To save you both the trouble of dirtying your hands?"

He blinks, confusion stealing over his face. Oh … he is good. Wide eyes, an innocent face. He has the whole act down fucking pat. I continue on, my words spilling out uncontrollably. "I know everything. How you two came to Sammy's specifically for me. How you knew everything about me before you ever stepped inside. How you're planning on killing me!" I finally run out of words, gasping for breath, tears starting their embarrassing streak down my face.

His face pales, and I'd look to Drew, but I can't pull my eyes from his. "Candace … that isn't … you think we're going to *kill* you?"

"Don't give me that innocent face," I hiss. "Did you guys think I was stupid? Did my low GPA put a giant 'Here is a Dumbass' sign above my head?"

"So … you're *not* suicidal?" Nathan seems stuck on this topic, ignoring my questions, color beginning to return to his face, an improvement that irritates me. He shouldn't be comfortable; he should be at least half as confused as I am.

"No, I'm not suicidal!" I snap. Part of me is pissed that they place enough self-importance on their own impact to think it would drive me to take my own life.

Drew pulls out a stool and sits, looking up at me. "The questions you were asking Nathan … about your father's care … it was because you thought we were going to kill you?"

I raise my chin defiantly and cross my arms, saying nothing.

He shakes his head, bewildered. "Why?"

I don't want to answer his questions. I want, for once in this fucking life as Candace Dumont, to get some answers. "Why don't you start by telling me the truth?" I look back at Nathan, who steps forward, his arms crossing over his chest, his unease gone, my dominating husband back in control.

"I don't owe you full disclosure. There are things you don't need to know."

"Bullshit!" I yell the word, startling him, and he shoots me a stern look, anger stealing over his face.

"No one is planning on harming you, I can promise you that. We aren't murderers. What even gave you that thought?"

I don't answer, biting my lower lip and considering my options. *Is this the moment? The time when I show my cards?* There is a risk in me showing all of my cards. It would give them an opportunity to craft lies around the evidence. It's too early for that gamble, especially when I can't figure out his involvement in this mindfuck of my life. I'm at the precipice between a good decision or disaster. I glance, from Nathan to Drew, and pick the weaker of the two opponents. I move closer to him, taking the adjacent bar stool and sitting down next to him. "I'm about to walk out that door and say 'fuck you' to any agreement I've made. I need you to tell me *right* now what is going on and why I am here."

He glances at Nathan, and I watch his eyes, watch unspoken words travel, and when he looks back at me, some decision has been made. "You asked me once why I am here." He moves his stool a bit closer, his knee brushing with mine. "You have your father. I have my sister."

I inhale. Not to be unsympathetic, but this sounds like a long story. I glance at Nathan, and the look on his face, the tight pinch of his features as he leans against the closest wall ... it kills any comments. My father ... his sister. I look back at Drew. "Is she sick?"

He shakes his head. "No one knows. We don't know where Cecile is. She disappeared, four years ago. From this house right here."

Cecile. The mysterious fiancée. Drew's sister? It's too much, my brain short circuiting, and I try to catch up on everything in the course of a breath. I shift slightly, not looking at Nathan, and lower my voice. "Did Nathan do something to her?"

There is a sigh of exasperation from Nathan's corner of the room.

Drew glances at him, and the corner of his mouth twitches in what is almost a grin. "Trust me, if I thought he had something to do with her disappearance, I would have strangled the truth out of him by now. No, Nathan wants to find Cecile as badly as I do."

I risk a look at Nathan, and catch the tight nod. I exhale, my first clear breath in a week.

Drew continues. "You're here for two reasons. The first is our ridiculous hope—if Cecile sees Nathan moving on—that she might come back."

Nathan looks down, his arms crossing over his chest, and I see in the tight press of his lips, the first hint there may be something vulnerable that exists in him. I look back to Drew. "And the second reason?"

Drew explains. A decade ago, a ten million dollar loan from Nathan's sister had been the funding that had launched his development business. One of his initial projects had been Casa Mar, a six hundred-room resort in Nassau. When Casa Mar finally sold out, Nathan set up a Bahamian account in his sister's name, transferring fifty million dollars into it—his repayment for the loan, plus his gratefulness in interest. His plan was to give her the account number on her next birthday.

Nathan steps forward, his voice cold, the vowels flat. "She died four days before her birthday." He spins my stool toward him, and leans in, resting his weight on the arms of it. "In a riding accident. You ask why we picked you?"

I lift my eyes to meet his.

"My sister was born on June 6, 1988. Her name was Candace Dumont." He pauses, letting the information sink in. "You're here because of the day you were born, and that passport that is coming in the mail. You will be, as far as that bank in the Bahamas is aware, the owner of her account, and I am planning on using you to make one hell of a withdrawal."

CHAPTER 36

I sit by the pool, dusk stealing over the yard, the lights of Nashville coming to life in the distance. A firefly glows, zipping by, and I follow its path. The understanding of why I am here brings enormous relief. First, in the form of safety, my mind back-flipping happy they are not plotting to kill me. Second, it illuminates my escape. I am here for a reason. If I perform as expected, I should be allowed to leave without penalty. I am in the new position of being able to negotiate my release. At this moment, I have the upper hand.

The motion sensors come on, and I look over, watching Drew step down the path and stop beside me.

"What are you going to do, Candace? Leave him?"

I cross my arms, hugging my chest, the night air suddenly chilly. "I don't know."

Putting his hands in his pockets, he turns and studies me. "He still loves her, Candace." He shifts, his shoes crackling against the pavers. "Cecile. He is still madly in love with her. It's why he is so cold with you." He glances out at the view and I stiffen, the slight hurtful in its truth.

"He's not cold," I say quietly. *Not always.* There are times, when his hands are in my hair and his tongue is soft against mine, that he is fully and completely engaged. It is a female's right to be possessive of those things that are hers. And he, as my husband, is mine.

Drew's jaw tightens, his green eyes returning to mine. "I just thought you should know. For Nathan, the moment he saw her—he was done for. It's one of the reasons he's still looking for her. She still,

175

four years later, has complete control of his heart. He will *never* stop loving her."

I look away, needing the space, my mind trying to decipher what my heart feels for Drew. He's speaking of Nathan, but I feel this is about us. And I can't even think about that. I regret ever kissing him. With everything I've just learned, my purpose here, his sister ... it feels like his seduction of me was a ploy, something to separate me from Nathan, to give his sister better footing, or some sick form of competition. I don't know what it was, and maybe it was innocent, but I can't deal with it, *with us*, right now. There should have never been an "us", and now that I understand Nathan's motivations, his behavior over the past two months is shone upon in an entirely different light. I push to my feet, ignoring Drew as I return to my room.

***

"Good evening."

The sound of Nathan's voice in my room is so foreign that it takes me a moment to place it. I turn from my place at the dresser, seeing him in the doorway, his tie loosened, shirt untucked. His hair looks like he has been running his hands through it all morning, his face lined, eyes tired. I feel a stab of sympathy and realize I'm already looking at him differently, my glasses rose-tinted with the new information.

It is the romantic side of me, the side who devours love stories, the side who still believes in soul mates and tragic love. That side is enamored by the fact that this man can still pine for the woman who crushed his heart. The man with the body of sin, who at the moment is scowling at me like I have taken his favorite toy and tossed it off a bridge. "Mark said you needed me?"

I stand and rest a hip against the dresser. "I have a proposition for you."

He raises his eyebrows. "We went through that already. Two months ago. Our business arrangement has already been settled."

"I'd like to renegotiate."

"With what?" He moves closer, his eyes sharp on mine.

"With my name. It appears that I have sole control over the funds in that account. I am happy to help you access it, but I want something in return."

"And what would that be?" He moves another step closer, and I forget how to breathe for a moment, the scent of him too familiar, bringing to mind too many memories of slick, bare skin and a hard, demanding cock.

"I want out. A divorce, or annulment, whichever is appropriate. But I need you to continue providing for my father. And I'd like a little bit of money to start fresh, somewhere other than Sammy's."

He frowns. "That's asking for a lot in exchange for two months of your time."

"And what was your original plan, after you got the money? Dump me with ten grand? Send my father back to the city hospital?" My body tightens in sudden anger. "You want to fuck with my life for three months and then toss me aside? I think that's taking a lot considering what you are getting in return." I reach forward to poke his chest and he grabs my hand, his grip tight on my skin.

"It's my money, Candy. I'm just getting it back. I'm not taking something that I don't deserve."

"You haven't answered the question," I glare. "What was your plan for after you got the money?"

He releases my hand. "I wasn't going to leave you. I was going to stay married."

"What?" I say, baffled. "Why?"

"What Drew said earlier is correct." He meets my eyes. "We're hoping a wife may provoke Cecile to return."

"Wouldn't a wife make her *less* likely to come back?" I would certainly write off an ex who remarried, the wedding proof positive that he had recovered, and gotten over me.

He gives me a wry grin, a casual gesture that makes my heart stop and my knees weaken. I think it's the first time I've ever seen him smile when it wasn't for the cameras. "You don't know Cecile. She is very competitive, very possessive. The thought of me with a young, beautiful woman … it can't hurt." He shrugs. "I've tried everything else."

"So you want to stay married?" The last few hours, my mind had been making plans for Life After Nathan. Staying married ... it was a thought that had never crossed my mind.

"Yes. Assuming, of course, you are willing."

I sit, wanting, more than anything, to put some distance between us. I can't function properly when he is close to me, his scent too sexual for me to ignore.

I block out his sex appeal and force myself to remember that I am miserable as Nathan's wife, the rules too constrictive, the control unbearably tight. I shake my head. "I don't think I can do that. At least not with how things are now."

He cocks his head. "What do you mean?"

"The rules ... how you are with me. I understand it now; you were keeping things from me and trying to keep me from having feelings for you ... but I am miserable."

He frowns. "Is it the sex or everything else?"

I hesitate. "Both, really. The sex ..." I blush, despite myself. My face should be immune to blushing, especially in the area of sexual conversation. And Nathan certainly doesn't seem uncomfortable. I swallow. "The sex is great, at least for me. I don't mind exhibitionism so much, but not in front of Drew—that bothers me." I try to say the words casually, try to not give away anything more than what I intend. "And ... that night." I shudder. "With that guy." I look up at him, my face resolute. "I will never do something like that again."

He nods, his eyes on mine, our gazes locked in a stare that I can't pull away from. "I'm sorry for that. I thought ..." He shrugs.

"I'd love to know the rest of that sentence."

His eyes harden, my tone one I have never used with him. But things need to change, our playing field to level.

"There were two reasons for that. One was because it turns me on seeing your mouth wrapped around another man's cock." His blunt words make me blink, the heat behind them causing a curl of desire in my belly. "Second, I did it to keep distance between us. To remind you that I was in control, and to stop you from harboring any illusions of romance."

That causes me to laugh, a short bark of disbelief. "Romance? Believe me Nathan, you have made that abundantly clear. I didn't need to suck a stranger's dick to figure that out."

He looks away. "I'm sorry." His gaze returns to me. "And there won't be anything happening in front of Drew. Now that you know everything, he'll be moving on." He chews on the edge of his mouth. "So you don't need to worry about that anymore."

Drew's leaving. A wave of relief hits me at the news, so many uncomfortable future moments, suddenly gone. No need to figure out our future, or lack of. No need to discuss what happened.

Nathan clears his throat, and I look up at him. "Thank you. For helping me. As far as the marriage and our agreement goes, I will think about modifying our marriage, but would like you to think about continuing our agreement, if I make some concessions to improve your happiness."

He steps closer, stopping just before me, and I lose all intelligence when his hands settle on my hips. "What kind of concessions?"

"Make a list of your demands," he says gruffly. "But sex is a non-negotiable. I can't be around you without having you." With that declaration, he pulls me closer, and lowers his mouth to mine.

I have learned so much about this man since our last kiss, the roller coaster of my emotions taking me through a year's worth of emotions in two short days. I respond, feeling the pull of arousal as my legs weaken and mind spins. I cannot say no to this man. His touch, his mouth. I grip the back of his neck as he lifts me by my waist, spinning us around and dropping me softly on the bed, the mattress sinking as he climbs above me.

As his mouth whispers down my neck, his tongue thumbing over the delicate skin, I wrap my legs tightly around him, pulling him closer, feeling the strength of his arousal against my needy body. I turn my head, opening the other side of my neck to him and see Drew— standing in the main house, his face dark with anger.

CHAPTER 37

I can live without romance. But the coldness from Nathan, that is what I have struggled with. That is what has made me feel the whore. The Nathan of today was different, smiling and carrying on a conversation without disdain, his charm and breeding causing my heart to do a subtle swoon. That Nathan—who spoke to me freely, listened to my words and treated me as an equal—that man I can live with.

I close my eyes, thinking of Drew, the expression on his face when our eyes met. When I saw him standing in the main house, watching us through the window, I turned my head, pushed his image out of my head and focused on Nathan's hands, which were sliding under my shirt, his strong hands on smooth skin, the nip of his mouth against my neck.

"What's going on, Candace?" My eyes flip open at Drew's voice. *Speak of the devil.* I turn and watch him enter my room, his hands in his pockets—a deceptively casual gesture, his shoulders tight with tension, mouth pinched.

I toss down my magazine. "Nothing. Knocking would be appreciated."

"Nathan didn't knock." The sharp tone of his words makes my guilt vanish and anger rise. He chuckles, a long, mean sound, and wanders through the room in a path that brings him closer to me. "Why'd you fuck him?"

I raise my chin, meeting his eyes. "I'm not your property, Drew. And, since you seem to be irrational, let me remind you that I am still bound by my agreement to Nathan."

He scoffed. "The rules are out the window. You know that, you knew that the minute that we told you about the money; hell, your eyes lit up like a neon sign. You have power now, you could have told him no. Things are different now."

I have power. I've told myself that fact, but it is different, hearing it from Drew. Solid. Concrete. I have power. I can fix this situation.

"Are you going to continue fucking him?"

I don't know what he wants. He's leaving. I'm staying. I have power, I don't have to be miserable. I can have my cake—Nathan—and eat it too. This new Drew, one with too many motivations, and not enough transparency—I don't like. I stand. "I don't think that's any of your business."

He leans forward, his hands fisting, making me think, for a brief moment, that he might lose control. "It is, in *every* way, my business."

I have to get away from him. His intensity is too strong, his need too great. He has no one else to consider, no other emotions to fight. For him it is simple, a masculine, caveman need to dominate another man's property. I see woman. I fuck woman. I own woman.

I see man. I fuck man. I desire romance.

The true epitome of romance is Nathan and Cecile. She disappeared, breaking his heart into a thousand pieces, yet he still loves her—pines for her, will not look at another woman in the same way, his heart completely captivated by a woman who cares nothing about his life. I know. I can see the distance in his eyes, the constant distraction, his inability to see anything other than her absence. He has needs—I've felt that need between my legs, felt it sweep through him, his cock fucking me as if I am his last breath, and he is dying without oxygen. But his need only controls his body. *She* controls his heart.

I see man. I fuck man. I want man's love.

Drew steps forward, pulling something from his back pocket and tossing it onto the bed. A small blue book, a gold seal on the front. "Your passport," he says shortly. "There is also a card with Candace's social security number and bank account number, both of which you need to memorize. The jet will depart day after tomorrow, *Mrs. Dumont.*"

I pick up the book, flipping it open to stare at my photo, my fingers tracing along my new name. I hear Drew's exhale, see the look he gives me as he turns and walks out. And I wonder, as the door slides shut behind him, if he will try and come to me tonight.

I lock the door.

CHAPTER 38

I open the closet, and flip on the light, scanning the shelves until I spy a matching luggage set, three red and black Diane Von Furstenberg vintage-style trunks. I carry them to the center of the room and open Rosit Fenton's book of outfits.

I flip through the pages, pausing occasionally and moving back to the closet to pull hangers. With each new item, laid out in neat stacks on the bed, I am reminded of how lucky I am. My fingers pluck through designers I've only dreamed of. Oscar de la Renta. Versace. Chanel. I scoop up a pair of Louboutin heels, and some Tory Burch flats. I place the items carefully in the trunks, then move to the bathroom, which has MAC's entire lineup, paired with every beauty item possible. Can I leave this life? Suddenly all of my complaints seem so trivial. *My husband is taking me to the Bahamas for a week in our private plane.* I let my eyes drift over the expensive details of the bathroom, the view of the sparkling pool and beautiful home. *This is my life.* I'd be foolish to leave.

I step to my desk, where my notepad sits, the page blank. I've tried a dozen times to do as Nathan asked, and write down my demands, to spell out what it would take for me to stay in this life.

I know what I really want. To sleep in bed at night next to Nathan. To have the Nathan who comes out when the cameras are on us— his loving smile, soft hands, mischievous grin and playful stories. I want to spend my evenings with him, side by side on the couch, my head in his lap, his hands in my hair, quiet moments that we both would treasure.

But I can't put those demands down on paper. I can't show my cards, especially not when it's a losing hand. The worst-case scenario is for him to give me all of that, while his heart is still Cecile's. My heart wouldn't be able to resist, would fall down a long dark hole that it would never be able to climb out of.

CHAPTER 39

"Ready?" Nathan settles in across from me, pulling the seat belt across his lap. I nod, and he calls out to the pilot, stretching his long legs forward as he settles in.

"I am. Thanks for pushing back the flight." Originally, we'd planned to leave this morning, but I'd had a sudden and frantic desire to see my father. I'd sped the entire drive to Crestridge, and had gotten in a full two hours with him before he was sleeping and I was headed back to the house. Now, we're flying to Fort Lauderdale, where we'll have lunch and fuel up, then continue on to Nassau.

"No problem. It gave me some time to knock out some work items. I needed to scout out a lot anyway. It's a hotel site downtown. Next week, if you are up for it, I'd love to get your take on it." He speaks so freely now, his cold demeanor warmed to an impressive 98.6 degrees. *Human.*

I smile at the observation, reaching into my bag and pulling out a water bottle.

"What?" He leans forward. "That smile is worrisome."

"Worrisome?" I laugh. "It's just weird. How quickly you become normal. You were so unfriendly before."

He frowns, adjusting his suit jacket, and smoothing down the lapels. "Like I told you, I didn't want you to get the wrong impression. I wanted to be sure you were aware what our relationship was about."

"Sex."

"Well … sex, and your new identity. But, as you know, we had planned on keeping that part from you." He says the words with a hint of an apology—not quite remorseful about his actions, but regretful of the deceit.

"And now, you feel comfortable with me? With me understanding that relationship?"

His blue eyes study my face, his shoulders relaxing at my calm demeanor. "Yes. I'm assuming, now that you know about Cecile, that you understand my ... inability to give anything more."

Cecile. I am really beginning to hate that bitch. I sigh. "So, tell me the plan."

It doesn't take him long to tell me, mostly because it is ridiculously simplistic. Originally, when I was to be kept in the dark, Nathan planned on taking me into the bank, with the pretense of opening a joint account in our names—presenting it as a token of goodwill. The paperwork would be simple, a registration card for the account, showing both of our names. I would sign, never knowing that, instead of adding both of our names to a new account, I was adding Nathan's name to a pre-existing account, one with a cool fifty million inside.

Now that I am aware of the con, the new plan is to do a simple funds transfer, from his sister's account to Nathan's. They will ask for identification, I will present mine, and everything should be done in a matter of minutes.

"Will there be any paparazzi?"

"Only in certain places. Mark's hired them for some restaurants and resort locations, so we can manipulate those occasions." He takes a tight curve on the road, looking over as he drives. "Are you comfortable with that? Being photographed with me?"

"You mean, as a ploy to get Cecile's attention? Yes, I am fine with that." I lean back, curling up against the seat and closing my eyes, keeping my face peaceful. I don't want any part in aiding a reunion between this man and Cecile. But, when he is acting, when he is playing to the cameras and grinning and leaning into me, planting soft kisses and holding my hand—that is heaven. And even if it is fake, even if it is for another woman, I'll take it.

CHAPTER 40

Our plane touches down on a tiny runway, the line at customs crowded with antsy vacationers. It takes over an hour to get through, a bored Bahamian stamping my crisp new passport with barely a glance.

The limo, sent from the Atlantis Resort, is laughable—a decade old Lincoln with worn seats, ripped carpet, and a back window held together by a strip of duct tape. I shoot Nathan a worried look and he grins, placing a gentle hand on my back and guiding me in to the car. "Don't worry," he says. "These guys are subcontractors for the resort. It will get better."

And it does. From the two hundred foot yachts cozied up outside of the towering casino walls to the gold columns, arched ceilings, and hand-painted murals decorating the lobby walls. We take the scenic route down to the pool deck, walking through a stone cavern of fish tanks, giant manta rays traveling alongside us. I try to contain my glee, to maintain an air of aloof snobbery, but fail miserably, shrieking with excitement as a shark swims by, and gasping at the beautiful actions of glowing jellyfish.

We cross a rope bridge over lazy hammerhead sharks, and when my feet sink into warm white sand, a tropical paradise of perfect blue green water before me, I can't help the grin that stretches over my face, taking up every square inch of real estate up. I wrap my arms around Nathan's neck, catching him by surprise, my lips pressing exuberantly to him, his mouth widening into a smile beneath mine.

"You like?" he whispers.

"I love," I shoot back, jumping up and wrapping my legs tightly around him, my momentum knocking him off balance and taking us down to the ground, my mouth pestering him for another kiss, his laugh catching us both off guard and giving me full access to his mouth.

The moment changes, heating up, his hands traveling down, roughly gripping my sundress-covered ass and pulling me against his body, the line of his arousal suddenly stiff against me.

The click of lenses is what pulls us out of the moment. He rolls with me, sitting up on his knees, gently brushing sand off of me and offering me a hand. I accept, and he pulls me up and in for one more kiss, a playful smile on his lips. "Let's go to the room," he says hoarsely, his eyes darkening. "I need you. Now."

And we run, sandy flip flops slapping against bare rock, my smile lasting through two elevators, one long ass hallway, and onto the giant bed in our luxurious penthouse suite.

CHAPTER 41

"Another beer?"

I look up from my plate with a smile. "Yes, thank you."

We are in Seafire, a steakhouse in the Atlantis resort, dining on lobster and steak at a table by the window. I can see cameras when I look outside, the collapsed arm of a photographer draped over a large lens, cigarettes glowing in the night as they chat, waiting for us to leave. Every once in a while I find their eyes on me, their lens positioning for a quick shot.

"Are you having a good time?" Nathan asks, tipping back an ice-cold bottle of Kalik.

"Considering all we've done is have one incredible fuck, yes. Thank you for asking, Mr. Dumont. Excellent trip planning." I grin, taking a mouthful of conch and settling back in my chair, savoring the buttery taste of perfection.

"Any qualms about tomorrow?"

"As a matter of fact, I wanted to talk to you about that."

His eyebrows rise questioningly. "Yes?"

"First, I just want to confirm that, upon our separation, you will continue to care for my father."

He settles back in his chair. "There is no chance of you continuing in the marriage?"

I brush off the question with a shrug and a swig of my beer. "I'll let you know that after this weekend. I need more time to think about that. More time with this …" I gesture with my fork. "…Nathan. I'm not used to him yet."

He grins. "Point well taken. I'll try not to bend you over in front of any strangers while we're here."

I frown, the joke hitting a little close to home, reminding me of my lips on a stranger's cock—Nathan's hand sliding up the back of my dress as I sucked. The problem was two-fold. I hated being used, being told what to do, but I had grown wet during the experience, his authoritative instructions incredibly erotic in their commanding tone. I try to refocus, to move my thoughts back to where I am, on my fairytale dream date. "Let's get back to my dad."

He shrugs, cutting into his steak. "You saw the amendment my attorney made. Your father is officially my life-long dependent. I will support any medical expenses while he is sick—once he improves, I will cover his living expenses, up to seven thousand dollars a month."

"I just want to make sure that you're okay with it; I don't want you to feel forced into anything."

"The money you are helping me recover will more than cover it. But thank you for your concern." He smirks, and it's the kind that makes me want to yank open his fly and suck his cock right here.

"There *is* a second condition," I say, dipping a piece of bread in olive oil.

"Yes?" he asks wryly.

"It involves our sleeping arrangements."

The laughter leaves his eyes.

"If you want me to help you tomorrow, then I want to sleep with you while we are here. Not in the second bedroom of the suite. In your bed."

It shouldn't be an outlandish request. It should be something he agrees to easily, without hesitation, considering the fifty million dollars at stake—a lifetime of wealth. But I can see from his eyes, from his tight jaw and the hesitation with which he speaks, that this is difficult for him.

"You want to sleep with me," he repeats. "That's your request?"

"Yes."

"Why?"

I shrug. "Ever since I moved to Nashville, I've felt…" *Like a whore.* The words sit on the edge of my tongue, only I'm too ashamed to verbalize them. "Disconnected from you. I feel isolated. If I'm going to stay in this marriage, I need to feel some sort of normality in our fake relationship." I grimace. "At least for a few nights."

He nods and the candlelight reflects in the blue of his eyes. "I understand loneliness. I ache for Cecile in a way that hurts. But, I want to make sure that you know—"

"I got the memo, Nathan," I interrupt him crossly. "You don't love me. Aren't going to love me. I hear it loud and clear. A fucking cuddle session isn't going to change that."

The response catches him off guard, a grin catching his mouth before he leans back and laughs. He shakes his head, taking a swig of beer before looking at me sheepishly. "I'm being a little conceited, aren't I?"

I grin. "A bit. You give one hell of a fuck, but yes, you aren't *that* tempting." A bald faced lie. Give a girl some time with this version of Nathan, and she could easily drown in his blue depths.

"Hey," he says with a devilish wink. "Back at'cha. In regards to the fucking, that is." He reaches forward and snags my hand, bringing it to his lips for a soft kiss. "As far as lovable, an unattached man would be insane not to fall for you." As he brushes that delectable mouth over my knuckles, my heart tries hard not to swoon.

I tug on my hand, trying to salvage my most crucial organ before it shatters into a million pieces. "Any other reasons you hesitate to open that sacred bed up to me?"

He hesitates. "When Cecile comes back, I want to be able to tell her that any other women—you or anyone else I've been with—meant nothing to me. That I've been waiting for her. That it has been purely sex with them, nothing more."

Aw fuck … My heart implodes, the sharp stabs of a thousand tiny emotions. I busy myself with lobster, taking out my aggression on an innocent claw, fighting to keep my face calm, and only half listening when he continues speaking.

"But, if it's important to you, I'll do it. I need this money. There is an opportunity in Puerto Rico and I need this capital to take advantage of it. Asking for two nights in bed is a small request on your part."

"And my father," I remind him.

"That part's easy," he says, taking the lobster from me and breaking it open with one carefree motion.

Great. A long-term financial burden is easy. Two nights with me—that's the part he finds difficult.

NATHAN

It's funny how your head can forget things. He looks in her eyes, glassy from the alcohol, a grin stretched across her face, and can barely remember Cecile's face. A woman once so ingrained in his thoughts, his mind so dominated by her absence, and now he can barely remember her smile. Candace smirks, and he leans forward. "What?"

"Oh ... nothing." She fiddles with her watch, a Tag Heuer that he had given her during the flight. Lined with diamonds, it was a small concession to the favor that she was, rather cheerfully, performing. "Just thinking about your Jekyll and Hyde tendencies."

He scowls, and she laughs. "I'm serious!" She reaches forward, touching his arm, and it's all he can do not to grab her wrist and pull her into his lap. "In Napa you were wonderful. Then we got back to Tennessee and you were ice cold. Now you're flirtatious and fun ..." she wrinkles her nose at him. "I'm just a little afraid of the monster that's lurking, once we touch back down on US soil."

He sits back, crossing his ankles, and pulls his beer toward him. "No monster anymore. Drew and I thought..." he tilts his head. "We thought it'd be easier for you if I was an ass." He lifts his beer to his lips and watches her struggle with a crab leg, her forehead pinching in concentration.

She glances at him. "So the asshole thing was all an act?" She sniffs, putting the edge of the leg in her mouth and cracking the shell with her teeth in a manner that would make Rosit Fenton shriek in dismay. "Nobody's that good of an actor."

"Fine," he snaps. "Maybe I enjoy being an asshole at times." It isn't exactly true. It wasn't that he had ever wanted to hurt her. But sometimes, he had needed some distance, needed her to step away, to lose that look in her eyes, the glimmer of hope he saw come through that curve of her mouth. Sometimes, he'd needed to cut her just to save his own neck.

She laughs, and he wonders if, maybe, this could ever be about more than just the money.

CHAPTER 42

An hour later, my heart has forgiven him, aided by a half dozen bottles of ice-cold Bahamian beer. The alcohol has loosened our tongues, words spilling across the table before either of us can hold them back. We have agreed, in one drunken toast, to open the vaults: freedom to ask any question and receive a full, unedited response. We started off friendly, but the questions have gotten dirtier and more personal as the beers keep coming.

Nathan flips a bottle cap in my direction. "Worst strip club client ever?"

I tilt my head. "My third week at the club, a husband proposed I join him and his wife for a threesome; I refused, the wife got offended, and sprayed me with a mini-Mace canister she had on her keychain. I looked like a crazy psycho-stripper for the next three hours, my eyes bloodshot and face blotchy." I grin at the memory, thinking about how close I came to quitting that night.

I bite my lip, looking at Nathan. "What's the story on Drew?"

He leans forward. "Drew was a cop. When Cecile disappeared, I hired him to look for her full time. When I told him about CeeCee—my sister—and her account, he helped to come up with the plan to create a new Candace Dumont, and he was the one who searched for a suitable woman with the correct birthdate. Once we brought you home, he was supposed to keep you under control. To keep you unaware." He snorts. "A job he failed miserably."

He dips a piece of lobster into butter and glances at me. There is something in his eyes, a question unasked.

I hesitate, wondering if I should tell him, the alcohol in my system pushing me forward. "I slept with him." I reach forward, grabbing my own piece of lobster. "I feel like you should know that."

I expect fireworks, his eyes to blaze, hands to fists, nostrils to flare. Instead, Nathan sighs, settling back in his chair. "Would you like to continue fucking him?"

I don't have to think about the question. "No."

"So, it's done with."

"Yes."

"Good." He pushes back, his chair sliding a few inches further from the table. "Now, come here." He pats his thigh.

"What?" I lift my beer to my lips, and giggle nervously.

"Candy." My name rolls off his tongue like silk, I can't argue with that look, the one that has issued so many delicious orders in the past. "I'm not going to do anything. Just come here." He pats his thigh again, and I stand, setting down my beer and making my way around the table, his arms pulling me down, until I am seated on his thigh. I steal a nervous glance at the rest of the restaurant.

"Kiss me," he commands, his hands sweeping up my thighs, and I pin my skirt down with my hands.

"Nathan," I chide.

"Kiss me."

I obey, and just the brush of lips reminds me of our chemistry, of the raw need that my body has for him. He takes a second one, then a third, moving off of my mouth and trailing kisses down my neck and onto my collarbone. I laugh, and he squeezes my side, and helps me back up with a groan. "Get back over there before you drive me mad."

"Yes sir," I mock, and his lips twitch, his fingers lingering on my thigh as I stand.

***

"I don't understand - when Candace died, wouldn't this account go to you as part of her estate?" We walk, hand-in-hand, past a line of yachts, the marina shops filled with tourists. Two kids run by us, shrieking, and we pause to skirt a family of four.

He grimaces. "She left everything to a local battered women's shelter. Because this account was unknown to anyone but me, the estate wasn't aware of it. I don't have a problem giving the shelter the ten million dollars I originally owed CeeCee. But the forty mill of interest that I tacked on... he sighs. "I'd like that back."

I nod, stumbling slightly on my heels and gripping his arm tighter. "And how does Mark fit into all of this?"

"You don't like to sleep alone; I don't like to be alone. A shrink would have a field day with that—and probably blame it on Cecile's abandonment. Whatever the reason, Mark handles most of the day-to- day business of the house and handles a lot of the overflow from my job—little errands that I don't have time to take care of." He pauses at a trash can tossing in his empty beer bottle. "Ever been in love?"

I shrug. "Nah. I haven't really met the right guy. A few crushes here or there. But the last three years haven't put me in the right situation. Most quality guys aren't interested in dating a stripper." I nod in his direction. "Case in point."

He winces. "Touché, my wife." The endearment rolls so easily off his tongue that we both startle at it. Then our eyes meet, and I smile. He leans forward, and with one gentle tug of his hand, pulls me to him for a kiss.

Spark. I can't kiss this man without my insides melting and my heart awakening. He deepens our kiss, his other hand stealing into my hair, tugging on the elastic band until my hair falls free. I grip his shirt, our mouths colliding in frantic passion. He pulls away, and I gasp for air. "Let's go. I fucking need you right now."

We hurry, my hand tight in his, up the stairs, through the casino, and into the elevator, where he takes me into his arms, my back against the wall, heart hammering in my chest. Then, the doors open, and a dozen steps later, we are in our suite.

I drop to my knees on the carpet, keeping him close, my mouth begging for a taste of his cock. He stops me, tugging on my arms, and I resist, looking up at him. "Nathan, I need this. Please. Sucking your cock has been on my mind for over an hour."

He looks down at me, his face heavy in need. "Trust me, I'm not stopping you. Move in front of the mirror so I can watch." He pulls me over until we are both before the large mirror, his hands unzipping and reaching into his pants, my heart leaping when all of him is before me.

Good Lord, he is magnificent. I move closer, devouring him with my eyes, barely feeling the tug of strings as Nathan undoes the ties that hold up my dress, the material pooling around my knees when he is done. I hold him in my hand, gently gripping it, feeling the skin move around hard bone, his breath inhaling sharply when I squeeze. I hold it up, the area around it neat and well-manicured, his obsession with control encompassing his nether regions as well, everything perfect, framing a package which I can't stop thinking about.

I start at his base, trailing my tongue along the veins and bulges of his organ, my eyes glancing up to find him staring straight ahead into the mirror behind me, his hands gathering my hair, his expression strong and possessive. "God, I love … everything," he groans, his eyes dropping to meet mine. "The curves of your back, the dimples above your ass … the feel of your wet tongue against my cock."

My tongue reaches the lip of his head, swirling around the base, and then I take it in my mouth, sucking it in and out, my hand gripping and tugging on his shaft, each downward pump hitting his balls. I move my hands, placing them on his thighs, tugging his pants down until they hit the floor, my hands sliding back up his bare legs as my mouth takes him deeper, wet sucks taking him to the back of my throat. He takes a fistful of my hair, holding me still and taking over the motion, thrusting quickly, then slowly. I look up into his eyes as he slowly withdraws, my lips tight around his cock as it leaves my mouth.

"You will be the death of me," he mutters, bending down and gripping my waist, lifting me easily up and walking me over to the bed. There, he repays me as we lay on our sides, facing each other. His mouth brushes my lips, kissing them softly, the hard length of him bumping tantalizingly against my legs as his fingers gently move over my pussy, teasing the velvet folds. My body arcs against him when he slips a crooked finger inside, a shot of electric pleasure that causes me to gasp, his mouth curving into a smile against my neck, as his finger brushes gently over the spot that was made for this. My inner walls contract and lubricate, the spot beneath his fingers swelling.

My fingers run down the planes of his body, traveling over the hard bone of his hip, moving down the V of his stomach until I reach my goal, my hands wrapping around him, my own mouth taking on a smile, my hand moving on its own accord, admiring the rigidness of his member as I explore its length. Our mouths find each other, a soft kiss turning deeper, our hands busy as we both move deeper into the sea of arousal.

I break the kiss, the intensity of my climax too great, my eyes clenching shut as my body tightens, a stream of words spilling from my mouth, the warm chuckle of Nathan only increasing the pleasure. My head drops back and I moan, a long guttural sound as sweet, pure intensity radiates out from deep inside of me, and it's satisfaction of the most intense kind.

I am coming down from my high when his fingers stop, pulling out of me and I feel the wide girth of his head, pushing through my folds and thrusting inside, my wet hot center ready, expanding and contracting around him as he pushes deeper inside. I wrap my leg around him and he rolls, putting me on my back as his cock fully buries.

There, he takes control, his breath ragged as his cock sets a firm rhythm, his intensity taking me, as it always does, by surprise. Hard thrusts let me feel exactly how aroused he is, every stroke bringing a new burst of pleasure.

I have fucked Nathan countless times. Standing, sitting, bent over or on his lap. But never this completely, never without an emotional wall of some sort between us, constructed either by him or me. This time, as his cock thrusts, as our eyes lock and our bodies move as one, my wall crumbles down.

In this moment, he takes my heart as well as my body.

***

The last time I spent the night with Nathan was in Rosemary Beach. I was a stripper, he a mark. I was already asleep when he got into bed, and he was dressed and gone by the time I woke. There was no cuddling, or spooning, no sweet words whispered.

When I crawl into the sheets, I almost expect the same. I lay on one side, facing away from him, and will my expectations into place. When the bed dents, and he slides up behind me, I hold my breath.

"Turn over."

I roll over, and he is there, gathering me against his chest, his leg hooking around mine, pulling me flush to him, and he gently lifts my head, sliding his arm underneath, until my cheek is against his chest, his heart thudding in my ear.

In the moments before his breathing deepens, his hold on me relaxing, it is perfection.

Forbidden. Impossible. Perfection.

PART FOUR

A woman's desperation is most clearly spoken in a kiss.

CHAPTER 43

I sit next to Nathan, giving him a nervous smile.

He reaches over, looping his fingers through mine, tugging a hand free and planting a soft kiss on the back of it. "Relax," he murmurs.

I try, letting out a breath and rolling my neck slightly to relieve the tension there.

"Mrs. Dumont!" The dark-skinned man strides up to me with a smile, reaching forward and enthusiastically shaking my hand. "I am Leo Brantling. It's a pleasure to meet you."

I match his smile, returning his handshake and gesturing to Nathan. "Mr. Brantling, this is Nathan Dumont."

The man turns to Nathan with a smile, repeating the greeting ritual. "Come, come. Let's step into my office."

His office turns out to be a small glass cube, right off the lobby, two worn chairs in front of a crowded desk. I had envisioned riding an elevator, walking through ornate halls and lobbies until we reached a large corner office. I set down my purse and shift uncomfortably in the chair.

"Now, how can we help you this morning?" The man looks to me.

"I'd like to transfer all of the funds in my account." I reach into my bag, pulling out the card that Nathan had given me two days prior, the account number written on the back.

"Will they be leaving the bank?" The man's eyebrows meet in a worried pinch above his brown eyes.

Nathan leans forward in his chair. "No, they will be transferred to my account, here at the bank."

"Very well." The man smiles. "Is that the account number?" When I nod, he takes the card, setting it before him and begins to type, his attention on the screen. "I'll need identification, preferably a passport, for both of you. Mr. Dumont, may I have your account number?"

As Nathan speaks, I pull out my passport, a slight tremor in my hands. My fingers smooth over the rough blue plastic, opening it slightly to see my new name staring confidently back at me. Candace Dumont.

I am Candace Dumont. I was born on June 6, 1988. It's all true. There's no reason for my hands to tremble, my heart to race.

"Mrs. Dumont, can you verify your social security number for me?"

My first lie. I recite the numbers, grateful for the time Nathan insisted I spend memorizing his sister's social. Then I hand over the passport, aware of the change in power that is occurring right here, right now. The weight of influence shifts with every dollar that transfers from Candace's account to Nathan's. After this, I will be expendable, my purpose fulfilled. No reason other than honor to keep his promises and care for my father, no matter what our contract may say.

It's done entirely too quickly, the whole process taking less than five minutes. $54,236,301.59 transferred from one person to another faster than a twenty-dollar lap dance. Nathan is unhappy with the amount, a scowl stealing over his face when he sees the figure. "What's wrong?" I whisper, scrawling a signature as I have been shown to do: a big, looping C followed by a swirl of squiggles, then the last name in clear, bubbly cursive.

He mutters something under his breath about the poor rate of interest and then signs the form. Inside, my stomach clenches. He should not have anything other than elation on his face, seeing as he is suddenly fifty-four million dollars richer.

We stand as a group, the beaming Bahamian shaking our hands and inquiring about our plans for the rest of the weekend.

Nathan loops an arm around my waist, bringing me to him. "We fly back tomorrow morning," he says, planting a quick kiss on my neck. "We just came into town for this transfer."

The man frowns. "You didn't have to come here just for that. If you have any transfers in the future, please know that we can easily handle that over the phone, provided that you fax or email us your identification documents."

Nathan winks, pulling gently on my hand, and we move toward the door. "I may have wanted to steal a few hours of her in a bikini."

"That, I can understand," the man says, flashing a smile as he holds open the door.

We step from the bank and onto the sidewalk, the flavor and sounds of Nassau all around us. As the doors close, my stress lifts. It is done; we have escaped, the money is transferred. Nathan grips my hand and smiles down at me.

"Are you happy?" I ask, holding up a hand against the glare of the sun.

"Ecstatic." He beams, pulling me to him and bending down to kiss me. "Thank you," he whispers, wrapping his arms around me and lifting me to his mouth, causing a squeal to leave my lips. A squeal he quickly silences with his mouth, spinning me in a small circle before releasing me. The limo, this one a small improvement over the first, pulls up, and he opens the door for me, gesturing with his hand. "After you, Mrs. Dumont."

I tilt my head graciously, a smile tugging at my lips. "Why, thank you," I drawl, ducking into the car and waiting for my husband to join me.

CHAPTER 44

We spend the day in town, walking through the shops of downtown, filling the car with shopping bags, and eating lunch oceanfront at a colorful strip of local eateries. In full view of the paparazzi, Nathan is the picture of a perfect husband, purchasing every item I touch and kissing me sweetly over fried conch and plantains. We walk into the hotel at four, dropping our bags inside the suite's front door, our hands on each other before the door even clicks shut.

He lifts me, wrapping my legs around his waist and carries me to the bed, our mouths fighting a frantic battle of ownership. When he bends, setting me softly on the bed, I pull back, taking a moment to study his face so close to mine. His thick brows rest perfectly above dark blue eyes, the color of deep water and just as dangerous, rimmed with thick dark lashes. His nose is slightly burnt, evidence of our time in the sun, the effect only reinforcing his All-American perfect bone structure. Those lips—full, pink, kissably irresistible. I reach up, needing him closer, needing confirmation that he is, in fact, here with me. That he is, indeed, mine in this one moment of time. I wrap my arms around his neck and pull him back down to my mouth.

Lust is a dangerous thing. It can seduce your mind and lead it blindfolded to the cliff that will be its demise. Nathan takes me to that cliff, my body bending and molding beneath his, my heart coming up for air in between soft caresses with his mouth while his cock hammers out a slick, rapid motion. I gasp, I arch, I dive. I'm not naïve enough to think that it's been lust this entire time. I've known what was sneaking in, looking for an opening and begging for admittance. But here, in this island paradise, sharing a bed and conversation with this beautiful specimen of a man ... here I can feel the final ties of restraint loosening, allowing the scary thing called love to work its way in.

The afternoon sun is streaming through our open window when he comes. The orgasm rips through him, his body heaving and bucking inside me, my name ripped from his throat as he gives a few final thrusts, his thighs trembling against my own as he buries himself fully inside of me.

I go limp, multiple orgasms turning my limbs loose and uncooperative. When he withdraws, collapsing beside me, it takes every ounce of my energy to roll over and curl up against his hard body. He moves me closer to him, dragging me higher until my head rests on his chest, his heart beating a strong rhythm in my ear, its steady beat soothing and secure. There, with his hand tracing a soft pattern on my naked back, I sleep.

***

I wake up to a dim room, the foyer light casting soft awareness over the room, the double doors open, an ocean breeze floating over the space. The crashing waves give the empty room a soothing presence. I lay there for a moment, listening, trying to sort out where Nathan might be. I have a faint memory of his arms lifting me, then setting me back down, the soft warmth of a blanket pulled over me, pillows placed under my head. I sit up, sliding the blanket back and standing, my eyes catching a note on the bedside table, my cell on top of it.

I'll be in the casino. If you feel up to it, please dress for dinner and come down. I'll be in the poker room.

ND

I set the note down, picking up my cell and pressing a button to illuminate the display. 7:45. I've slept for almost three hours. I move to the closet and turn on the light.

***

I find Nathan in the poker room, his face grim and chip stack low. He looks up, a smile crossing his face and rises, gesturing with a hand for me to come closer. When I reach his side, he pulls me onto his lap, kissing my neck gently and throwing in his hand. "I'm going to cash out," he says to the dealer, his eyes sweeping the low neckline of my dress, his hand smoothing down the side of my waist and affectionately squeezing my curves. "Did you get this one today?" he asks, tugging on the dress.

I nod. "How do you like it?"

"Absolutely stunning. Half the room noticed you come in." He runs his fingers up my back. "You hungry?"

"Starved."

"Then let's eat."

We step into an upscale Japanese restaurant just off the casino floor, and sit at the bar, ordering sake bombs and sushi. The restaurant is crowded, and we sit close, our arms touching, the heat of his body close to mine.

The sake is cold, the sushi delicious, and I relax, allowing myself to notice the light in his eyes, the ease in his manner, his good mood obvious in every smile, laugh, and touch. We touch frequently, his hand stealing to my knee, slipping salaciously underneath my dress, a soft kiss on my shoulder, my hand gliding into his hair, a stolen kiss over sashimi.

We stay until almost ten, stories and discoveries bubbling out, our different worlds having more in common than we thought. We are both David Baldacci fans, both love Scrabble, both grew up around horses, and are allergic to pine nuts. He promises to take me skiing; I swear I'll out-grill him in a steak-off. He wants a dog, and I promise to start researching a breed with rugged masculinity. We both think Beth is a bitch, and he promises to fire her upon our return. And he pays me the best compliment of the night, over gourmet fortune cookies, his face serious, eyes soft.

"You're a lot like her."

I tilt my head at him. "Who?" I am both terrified and hopeful that he would say *her* name. Cecile. The woman who so carelessly tossed aside the heart I covet.

"My sister. CeeCee. She was so wonderful, Candy. I wish you could have met her. She had a fire in her that glowed. It showed when she was pissed—God she could set fire to half the town when she was upset. But as mad as she got, she loved even fiercer. She was my other half. It was she and I against the world—even scarier—against our family. What she did for me? When Cecile left? She's the reason I made it through that at all. She fortified me, picked up my pieces and put me back together. You have her strength, her compassion, her fire. You're the only woman I know worthy to have her name." He looks sadly at me, his mouth turning up in a smile that doesn't reach his eyes.

I lean forward and tug on his shirt until our lips meet; communicating through my kiss what I am not woman enough to say.

NATHAN

Candy sleeps beside him, tucked against his side, her arm limp and soft across his chest. He needs to move her, his shoulder cramping, but can't. He can't risk waking her, her opening her eyes and looking at him in the darkness. Her eyes do him in. They see through every ounce of pretense and stare into his soul. He leaves her where she is, her body tight to his.

He is unraveling, the world that he knows slowly coming apart at a time when it should be coming together. He has control of the funds, transferring them through four different accounts to ensure their safety, their location one that only he knows—the IRS none the wiser about his regained wealth. His money is back, and now he is only missing one thing, the woman who took his heart. She is the last remaining piece of his happiness, and Candy could be the ticket that brings her back. Candy is playing along—smiling and acting the part of the devoted wife, madly in love with her husband, the photographers catching every flirtatious glance, every stolen kiss. Cecile's jealous streak is legendary, showing its teeth at several points during their relationship. She shouldn't be able to lie quietly, the photos and the press should flush her out, her ego demanding that he leave Candy at once so that she can go to bed happy, her pride still intact. It is a weak card, but the only one he has to play. Searching for her hasn't worked, Drew's extensive search bringing up nothing, his desire to find her as strong as Nathan's own.

What he can't figure out—what plagues him in the dark of the night—is why. Why did she leave? She left him, Drew, her family and friends, all for what?

He shouldn't want her back. He should curse her name, hate her photo, lament the day that she ever walked into his life. But he can't. She owns his heart, her touch imprinted on every ounce of his being, breath in his body, blood in his veins. Without her, he is lost.

CHAPTER 45

I know that Nathan's act is all for show, our Napa trip proof of that. The tender touches, the kiss on the nape of my neck—it is all for the cameras. *For her.* The fact that every touch that I swoon over is performed for another woman ... it's heartbreaking. Literally. I can feel my heart expanding, cracking along ridges and junctures, its shell not made to be manipulated, twisted, and toyed with in this manner. It bends, it yields, it cracks. I must do a better job of protecting it. I must push away from this man and focus on what is important. My father. The life I will have after Nathan Dumont.

But there is another possibility, another option in this game of Life that I am so poorly playing. After all, he is my husband. Maybe it's time to take off the gloves and pull some hair. I am here with him, she is a memory wrapped in abandonment. I have a fighting chance. I just need to time and properly place my blows.

***

We stand in the line at customs, Nathan's hand casually slid into my back pocket, occasionally tugging me to him for a kiss. I am wearing one of my new outfits, picked without the benefit of an outfit book or numbered hanger. It feels rebellious, choosing my own clothes, the simple act bringing a grin to my face.

This morning I threw away the notepad, its white surface damning my mind into a catatonic state, unable to create a single word of clarity. Besides, my needs are simple, no need for a physical list.

Move in. I want to live in the main house, to feel like a member of the marriage rather than a sequestered leper.

215

Sleep in his bed. I want his arms around me at night, his breath on the back of my neck, the hard line of his muscles within easy reach.

Sex. I will not fuck in front of others. Period.

A job. I'd like to fill my days with something other than waiting, the long drone of expectation too hard on my psyche.

That is it. Four demands. I'll ask him on the plane, once we are settled in and away from everyone. I want to have his answer, to have a plan in place, before I step off the plane.

CHAPTER 46

I watch his profile, wishing I was across from him instead of next to him, so I could study his face without being so blatantly obvious.

"It's been a good trip." He stretches his legs out, one reaching into the aisle, and leans back, turning to look at me.

I nod, a spot of silence beginning, the perfect opening for me to speak. "I've been thinking … about our marriage. And whether or not I will stay."

"And?"

"You asked me to make a list of things I would need. There are only a few."

He nods, staying silent.

"I want to live in the main house and sleep in your bed. Out in the guesthouse, by myself, I feel more like an employee of yours, someone you fuck and then disregard. It's not a situation I want to continue."

"And the sleeping? Couldn't you move inside without spending every night with me?"

I hesitate. Part of my demand was a negotiation tactic. Ask for more than I need, in hopes that he will settle where I want. I didn't *have* to have the nights. But I wanted them, had treasured every second of the last two nights. Plus, if I planned to fight for this man, I would need those evenings as part of the seduction of his heart. "Maybe not every night, but at least two a week."

"Before I commit to that, what else is there?"

A small grin pulls at my mouth. "Sex. You'll have to keep your controlling habits behind closed doors."

He laughs, pulling my hand to his mouth and nipping it slightly. "But I love taking your body before an audience. Love to see them watch you fuck." His words turn dangerous as he speaks, the light behind his voice turning to sizzling heat, his mouth on my hand a brand that marks me as his.

"Why?" I stammer. My eyes close slightly as he flicks a delicious rhythm on the meat of my palm with his tongue.

"It's how you look when you fuck, when you are unrestrained sexually." He drops my hand, the break in connection sudden, my mind racing to recover without showing anything on my face. He turns in his seat, fully facing me, his eyes latched on to mine. "That first night, when we came into the club ... I was only supposed to talk to you then—supposed to pitch you on a life of glamour and whisk you away. But it was how you looked under the lights. How you danced for me, the sexuality breathed out of you like it was part of your soul. I wasn't supposed to use you that night, to have you ..." He pauses, his voice roughening. "... suck my cock, but I couldn't help it."

His erotic words send a spike of arousal through me; the dark and confident look in his eyes makes me want to unzip his pants right here.

"I didn't know what to do after that, so I left, thought I'd come back the second night and have more control." His mouth curves. "Turns out my self-control, around you, is terrible."

"I want you to be the only one who watches ... at least for a while. Until I find my own footing in our relationship." I lick my lips, focusing on my words. "It's important to me."

He reaches out, cupping my face in his hand and rubbing a thumb over my moist lips. "I never meant to make you uncomfortable. And I can keep our sex behind closed doors; you don't have to ever do anything more than that. I just wanted to explain why I had enjoyed fucking you like that. Part of it was the control, my desire to keep you emotionally distant. But the other half of it, my personal arousal ..." His voice drops to a growl, the desire in it tangible, and he pushes gently on my mouth, his eyes closing as I open my mouth and gently bite on the meaty pad of his thumb. "I want to make you happy, Candy. I'm sorry I made you do those things."

I say nothing, the emotion in his eyes enough for me. He's sorry, and an apology was more than I ever expected. I gently release his thumb from my mouth, smiling at him.

"Was that it? Just those three things?"

I nod, figuring that I can bring up the job at a later day, the bulk of my needs covered in those three requests. He looks down, running a hand over his mouth and then studies my eyes, his dark blue depths searching me.

"If you stay ... if you continue to act as my wife ... I'll make those concessions. But we need to have more public exposure, and some high profile interviews and photo shoots at the house. I need to draw Cecile out, need to push our relationship into her face."

A smile breaks out, my excitement too great to contain, the mention of Cecile a small price to pay for such forward progress. His own mouth twitches in response, and he reaches out, wrapping an arm around my shoulder and pulling me to him, planting a soft kiss on my head.

"It'll be tough," I mumble into his chest. "But I'll pretend to like you. At least when the cameras are rolling."

He pulls back, using his other hand to tilt up my chin, his blue eyes smiling down at me. "What a good wife you are. Thank you, Mrs. Dumont."

I don't respond, my witty comeback lost as his mouth closes on mine, a soft kiss that deepens, my body relaxing and sinking into his embrace, my heart nose-diving after it.

His lips ... they are incredible.

CHAPTER 47

I feel like I have started a new journey in my life. Yes, it is strange and twisted—the two of us living together as husband and wife. He does it in a desperate attempt to win back the woman he loves. For me, it's an equally desperate attempt to corral the man who is stealing my heart. Even if he doesn't fall in love, being with him, feeling his hands on my body, his eyes on my soul, his laugh on my lips ... that will be enough. I am not that different from the woman who stood on stage two months ago. I wanted an escape, and I got one: complete with money, a renewed relationship with my father, and a devastatingly gorgeous man—a man who has turned out to be charming, funny, and a sexual beast in the bedroom. Even if he can never fully be mine, this life is more than I ever expected.

I suddenly understand why a woman would stay with a cheating man. It seems better to be happy with someone you love and overlook the fact there is someone else. Better than your thoughts and heart aching for them while you live a life alone. And I don't have the additional influence of a family—round, adorable children who climb into Nathan's lap and call him Daddy. It's just me, with a man that I can't stay away from.

I look out the window as the plane dips below the trees and our city comes into focus. North, along the rolling hills, I see our neighborhood, landscaped squares with mansions squatting possessively on blue-green lawns, gates and pavers directing the rich as they go about their worry-free lives. *Home.*

I turn to Nathan. "Drew has already moved out?"

He nods. "Yes, Mark's already confirmed that." He leans forward, squeezing my hand. "It works out well, he was staying in the second master suite, which will be more appropriate for you than one of the guest rooms. The housekeeper has already moved your closet over there, I thought you'd prefer to move your personal things."

I nod, settling back in the seat. I'll be sleeping in Drew's bed—his scent, his touch, everywhere around me. It's something I'm not sure fresh sheets and cleaning products will remove.

The plane shifts beneath us and I watch the airport come into view.

***

Mark is outside, waiting, when Nathan pulls into the drive. I step out of the car and stretch, surprised when Nathan comes around the car, his arm encircling and pulling me tight. "Money has been transferred, and I convinced the Missus to stay, to put up with me for a little while longer. Things are coming together."

He leans down, kissing me on the top of my head, his hand sliding down to cup my ass. Only home for seconds, but I can already feel the need coming off him, his fingers gripping me possessively. I blush, glance up at Mark, who smiles, and pulls a trunk from the car.

I'm brought back to attention by Nathan's hands, sliding around to the side of my leg, his fingers teasing the edge of my shorts, and I glance up at him. "Did you need something from me?" I ask, painting my face into a mask of innocence.

A smile tugs at his mouth and he laughs, bending and sweeping me into his arms. "I'm going to take my beautiful wife to bed," he says to Mark, pulling me to his mouth for a kiss. I shriek as he moves, my body bouncing in his arms, as we go up the steps, his eyes on me hungrily, his mouth curved into a smile.

Could it be? Will vacation Nathan be sticking around? My heart soars at the possibility.

He carries me to his bed, a space we rarely use, our sexual sessions kept to unromantic, highly visible places. Tossing me onto the duvet, he yanks at the collar of his shirt, pulling it over his head with barely contained excitement. "You mentioned me needing something?" he growls, the shirt tossed aside, his strong chest exposed, abs firm, his hands frantic at his belt. "Right now, I need to worship you with my cock."

I move quickly, matching pace with his movements, wanting, needing, to have him bare inside me right now, dominating me, the joining of our bodies in raw, unprotected union. He is fully naked by the time I have my shirt off, his strong, lean body crawling onto the bed, fully secure in its nakedness, his hands unbuttoning my shorts and tugging them and my panties off and down my legs.

A pause. His eyes survey my body, and I drink in the sight of him naked, kneeling in between my legs, his eyes black with need, his cock hard with arousal. It bobs straight out, my mouth watering with the urge to suck its hard length.

"You are so beautiful," he groans. "I want to do so many things to your body." He reaches down, his hand wrapping around his length, moving up and down his shaft. I reach my own fingers down, needing something inside of me right now, my need too great to go unsatisfied.

He chuckles, stopping my hand, moving it aside as his fingers brush against my heat, dipping inside one digit, then two, his eyes closing briefly. "Jesus, Candace. You are so ... perfect. So hot and tight. Always ready for me."

I arch on the bed, grinding against his fingers, needing them deeper, thicker, my eyes locked on his hard length, the erotic view of his hand on his cock, his eyes on me, his mouth open in unrestrained lust.

"I should have fucked you that first night," he groans, moving his cock down, his fingers out, the head of him hovering at my opening, his hands gripping my legs as he pushes inside in one smooth motion. He withdraws slowly, watching our union as inch by inch he pulls out, my body weeping at his exit. "If I had known then how perfect you are, I never would have passed on that opportunity. You are too amazing to not fuck at every ... available ... opportunity." He pulls the final inches out, my back arching, my eyes begging, his fingers resuming their penetrations.

"You assume I would have been willing," I gasp out, a smile across my face.

He tilts his head, possession in his eyes. "Do you think you could resist?" He positions himself back at my entrance, rubbing his head up and down my wet slit, easing in slightly, then pulling out, taking his stiff head to my swollen clit, brushing it gently.

"Of course," I breathe.

"Bullshit. By the time I finished with you, you would have been begging for my cock." His smug tone backs up his words, his cock pulling away from me as he strokes it again.

"Is that so?" Everything in me is centered between my legs. I have forgotten how to breathe, how to move, to think, to do anything but have this man fuck me back into reality.

"You tell me." He grabs my legs and lifts them so that they point to the sky, spread and open for him, his unrestrained cock finding its way straight to the source of my need. "Do you need this?"

I stay silent, my stubbornness combining with the curiosity of wondering what he will do next.

He moves his hips, the head of him entering, then withdrawing, my need rising and falling and rising as he fucks me with short, half-strokes, his mouth brushing against my calf, his tongue tickling out a pattern against my skin.

I groan, trying to slide closer, to get more of him inside me, the pleasure just short of enough, my orgasm reaching, straining, but not making the connection.

"Do. You. Need. This?" He grunts out the words, every other dip of his cock deep, then shallow, then deeper.

"Yes!" The word explodes from me, a plea for help in a deep hole of pleasure. "So fucking badly, Nathan. *Please.*"

He shakes his head, keeping his thrusts short, keeping me hovering on the brink of insanity. "Tell me that you are mine. To use as I wish."

I whimper, an ache inside me that is almost painful in its intensity. "I am yours. You are everything."

He moans at the words, dropping my legs and moving above me, his movements now unrestrained—full, deep thrusts that arc me higher, higher, higher. His face close to mine, features tight, breath ragged, fast movements that put his cock exactly where, exactly when, and exactly *how* I need it.

My orgasm hits—a blinding, waving curve of pleasure, peaking and falling, every thrust bringing me a fresh hit of sensation, breathing life and keeping its momentum, the moment impossibly long, then I am nothing but languid pleasure.

He doesn't stop, the drilling force of him bringing me back to the present, my legs wrapping around and gripping the hard muscle of his ass, my hands clutching and nails digging into his back, our bodies meeting in perfect orchestration until his eyes clench. He grunts, giving me four deep, hard thrusts, the proof of his finish shooting inside of me, physical heat pooling as he shudders and then is still.

"Fuck …" he whispers, hovering above me, his eyes on mine, wonder in them. "You have no idea how incredible that was." He rolls off me and onto his back, his cock pulling out, my body wanting it the moment it is gone. I roll over, curling up against his side, my hands unstoppable in their quest to touch, my fingers trailing up and over the lines of his abs, settling and stopping against his chest, his heart pounding beneath my palms.

"I didn't do much," I say, closing my eyes. "I just laid there."

"You don't have to do much," he says groggily, his mouth pressing gently against my hair. "You do me in with just a smile."

We are lying there, naked and half asleep, when the door opens and the end of my world walks in.

CHAPTER 48

She is beautiful, but I already knew that. The day after Drew told me about Cecile, I went to the library and used one of their computers. My hands felt foreign on the keyboard, the mouse awkward in my hand. Photos of them were all over the Internet—dominating old society articles, charity postings, and Facebook mentions. Our trip to Napa, the paparazzi shots of us at events—it is a drop in the bucket compared to their two years together. And as gorgeous as she looked in those photos, it pales in comparison to the woman standing before me.

Blonde, with green eyes that match Drew's, golden skin that highlights a thin frame, statuesque face, and soft lips. Lips that are parted, eyes that are wide, perfect breasts that heave as she gasps, her eyes darting from Nathan to me. Nathan to me. Her eyes grow wet, the dewy effect only making her more fucking beautiful.

"I'm so ... sorry," she stammers. "I didn't think ... I should have knocked ..." She lifts a shaky hand to her mouth, and turns, stepping toward the hall before looking back, anguish filling her face, and then she slumps. Eyes closing, knees collapsing, crumples to the floor, in the most graceful faint I have ever seen. Nathan jumps, finally in motion, rushing to her side, kneeling there at the same time that Mark appears in the doorway, his face tight.

"Did someone ..." His voice fails when he takes in the situation, his eyes zeroing in on the limp blonde, sinking to his knees, his hand grabbing hers.

I leave the three of them in the large master, sneaking past their threesome and to the opposite side of the house. Nathan, with his beautifully nude, hard body, bending over her and uttering soft words of love. Mark, elevating her feet, his figure running to the kitchen for a glass of water. Cecile, in the middle of it all, her beautiful features slack, breathing soft, blonde hair tangled around Nathan's fingers.

I enter my new room, walk naked to the bed, and sink onto it. My world zeroes in on that image, her one easy reentry into a life that I had *just* made my own.

I don't think there are enough words to describe how much I hate that bitch.

***

It was cruel for my mind to ever convince my heart that I had a chance. Of course she came back. Who wouldn't? But then again, who would ever leave Nathan to begin with? I tell myself that I didn't have enough time—that if I had longer, a few years, I might have been able to wrangle his heart, erase her memory, make him my own.

But it hasn't been long enough. And with her here ... I know what is coming. I know it despite the heated words I hear from my side of the house. I know without looking, without waiting, what Nathan will do. He loves her in a way that I can only dream for. Unconditionally, the hold she has on his heart tight and complete. He lives for her, works for her, breathes for her, loves for her. There is no one else in his world, no room for anyone else in his heart. I should have known, should have stopped my heart from skipping down fairytale lane, planting expectations, hopes and dreams that will never receive any nourishment.

I open Drew's old closet, and step in, looking through my racks of clothes and wonder what to take—what I have a right to. She won't want my clothes, won't wear the hand-me-downs. But she's a woman. We are possessive, territorial. I can't see her sitting by and watching me cart a fortune of clothes out the front door.

I grab a small Vuitton duffel and ignore the designer threads, throwing a few pairs of jeans and five or six of my favorite tops inside, dressing in something similar, lacing up tennis shoes and pulling my hair into a ponytail. I am zipping up my makeup bag, examining a Tag Heuer watch that Nathan gave me, when darkness blankets the room, a large form blocking the sunlight.

"I like you better naked." There is a smile in his voice. A *fucking* smile, at a time when my heart is hanging by threads in my chest.

I force my own lips to curve, command my voice to be light. "Most men do."

He steps inside, walking over to me. I want to tell him to stop. I try and force my legs to back away, my head to turn, but I can't. I just stand there, helpless, and wait for more heartbreak. He sighs, leaning forward and resting his forehead against mine, exhaling a slow, long breath of … what? Frustration? Anguish? A hopeful little voice in my head adds regret to the list of improbable translations.

He pulls back, lifting his chin and planting a soft kiss on my forehead, holding the contact for a heartbeat longer than necessary, my heart rising and soaring on the pipe dream of what he might say.

"I don't know what to say," he says softly. "I don't want you to leave."

Hope, a thin painful strand of it, glows.

"It doesn't seem fair to you."

His pity hits in a way that hurts. I step back, out of his embrace, and turn to my bag. I try to laugh, and it comes out strangled. "It's fair, Nathan." I stuff my makeup bag into the duffel. "We both knew what this was."

I don't ask him why he is taking her back. I don't ask him if he struggled with the decision, if I entered his head, if I was ever anything more than a pawn in the Get Cecile Back Game. I don't ask the questions, because I am afraid of the answers. I am afraid of more pity, afraid of kind words, and afraid of the truth.

Instead, I pick up my bag, and flash him a smile that would have made Rosit Fucking Fenton beam with pride. I smile, I wave, and I walk out of his life.

CHAPTER 49

Mark pulls up my car, idling it next to a bright white Maserati that must be hers. He steps out, and pops open the trunk. "Where are you headed?"

I blink at Mark's questions. Where indeed? I stepped out the front door intending to go home, but where is home? I haven't missed a single part of the life I deserted.

"Oh." Mark dips back into the car, and pulls out my old purse. "This is yours."

I unzip the purse and peek inside, pulling out my old cell phone. There is a new charger for it in the purse, a bit of thoughtfulness from Mark. I wonder how long ago he purchased the charger, how long he has been expecting to return my items and send me on my way. I turn on the phone, the battery charged, and scroll through numbers, each one a reminder of how sad and empty my old life was. I don't want to reconnect with any of them, and I'm pretty sure the emotion goes both ways. I turn it off, and push it back inside.

"I'm not sure," I announce. "But thank you for all of your help."

We hug, an awkward move between two strangers, and then I am in the Mercedes, watching the gates open, and exiting this life.

At the first gas station, I pull over, putting the car into park and re-opening the purse. Pulling out the contents, I examine foreign objects from a life I barely recognize. A sequined thong, the color garish, material rough, its cheap fabric causing me to wince in recollection of how far I had fallen in life. A tube of blood red Maybelline lipstick. Mascara. Tic Tacs. The keys to my house, my car.

There is an envelope, the handwriting on the front neat and tidy. Not Nathan's. I open it, sliding out a plain white card and a thick wad of bills.

Candace,

The items from your house are in a storage unit in Destin, the rent is paid through the end of the year, and the address is below. Doris is the manager; she can provide you with a key. Your car was sold, the cash from the sale added to your departure funds, which are enclosed. You will need to arrange payment for your cell phone; we have covered that bill during your time with Nathan. I will call you once the paperwork is in place for the divorce. Please do not change your phone number; we will need to stay in contact with you until this process is complete. After that, there will be no need for future contact.

Mark

I read the note twice, surprised at the coldness I feel in its parting. *There will be no need for future contact.* I don't know what I expected. An invite to their wedding? Baby showers?

I flip through the cash, counting it—fourteen thousand, five hundred dollars. Generous considering my Subaru couldn't have fetched more than a thousand dollars. Skimpy considering that our marriage earned Nathan so much.

I return the cash to the envelope and place it, and the cell phone, in the glove box. Rolling down the window, I pull up to a trash can and drop the purse, and all of its contents, into the can.

Then I pull out, and head to my father.

***

Dad is doing well, his improvement holding steady, which only means he is toeing the right side of death's line. I sit and hold his hand, my heart lifting when he opens his eyes and smiles at me.

"Go back to sleep," I whisper. "I'll be here when you wake up."

"It's not Wednesday," he says in confusion.

I smile. "No. I'll be here more often now. I'll explain it later. Go to sleep."

I *need* his sleep. I need to look over and see him in serenity while I make sense of the fucked up reality that is my new life. I feel Pam at my side and look up.

"Did something happen?" she asked, taking the seat to my right. "With you and Mr. Dumont? You both looked so happy in the Bahamas." Her face is tight, and I realize that she has been living my fairytale right along with me, the tabloids her peephole into our world.

I sigh. "Yes." I can't generate much more conversation than that, and she takes her cue and lets me be.

CHAPTER 50

I check into a Residence Inn three blocks from Crestridge, and spend the first few days at my father's side. He is overjoyed about the constant companionship, but seems worried, his watery eyes often on me, his mouth frowning without him even aware of it. Whenever I catch him watching, he straightens, fixes his mouth into a smile, and reaches out to grip my hand.

I will tell him soon. I just can't right now. It's too soon, and I won't be able to speak without crying.

Today, I have a meeting with the billing department at Crestridge, then a realtor. I need to find an apartment, preferably one with room for my father—should he ever improve enough to leave the hospital.

I pull into Crestridge, following the long, curved drive, my eyes picking up on all of the details that combine to create exorbitant billing. A huge gated estate with acres of gardens and rolling lawns, in an area known for high property values and ridiculous taxes, the security guard who waves me through with a familiar hand. The building, a complex that houses four floors of cutting-edge medical technology, a cafeteria that puts Ruth's Chris to shame, and a patient-to-staff ratio that defies all financial logic.

I am reminded, with every glance, at how much this all costs. I am reminded of Nathan's obligation, and my fear that he will default on our contract. I park in front of the building, and reach for my purse, willing my nerves to still.

Third floor. The elevator doors open to a place that reeks of obligations. I am cheerfully greeted by a receptionist and ushered to Mr. Hinton's office.

The man, one tall and thin enough to be a basketball player, looks up with a smile, taking off his glasses and standing to shake my hand.

"Mrs. Dumont, it's a pleasure to meet you. I take it that you are here to confirm the payment?"

I pause, halfway to my seat. "The payment?" I hadn't exactly had a clear reason for coming, other than to find out the status, and current balance, on my father's account.

He tilts his head, squinting at me slightly. "Yes. I assumed you knew. Your husband called earlier, and made a payment on Mr. Tapers's account."

Your husband. The title stabs me in a way that I thought I was insusceptible to. I settle into the seat and force a smile. "Mr. Hinton, you should know that Mr. Dumont and I are separated, soon to be divorced, though I hope that he continues the payments on this account."

He shakes his head slightly. "There shouldn't be any future payments. Mr. Dumont made a deposit that should cover at least three years' worth of treatment."

My mouth drops open. "Three years?"

"Yes. It's a little unorthodox, but should your father's health improve to a level where he can leave, I assured him we would refund him the credit."

I hate him for this. I hate him for keeping his promise, and giving me another reason to love him. My fear had been something to lean on, to hold against him in the lonely night when my heart is weak. I should be happy that he's kept his promise. But I feel sick, disgusted with the weakness of my heart and the inability to block him from my mind.

His mouth on mine.
His body over me, hands upon me, the trail of his fingers across my skin.
His eyes when they soften and look at me like I am whole.
His voice when it grows gruff and intimate, when it says words that make me swoon.

I thank Mr. Hinton for his time, and stand, moving unsteadily down the hall toward the elevators.

NATHAN

She sits at the bathroom counter, sitting forward at the chair, her face close to the mirror, a makeup brush in hand. Her hair is down, in blonde ringlets that lay against her bare back.

He sits back against the counter and watches her, his arms crossed over his chest. It is so foreign to have her here. To smell her perfume, to watch the familiar curves of her body step from the shower, to hear the gasp of her breath when he pushes inside of her. He straightens, moving off the edge of the counter and toward her, stopping behind her, his hands threading through the strands of her hair. She flinches, moving away from him. "Stop, you'll mess it up."

He doesn't stop, his fist closing on the bulk of it, giving a strong tug that pulls her chin upright, her eyes meeting his in the mirror. "Stand up." he says quietly. "Turn around and sit on the counter."

"What?" she laughs, pushing to her feet and untangling his hand from her hair. "Nathan, please. We're going to be late for dinner."

A memory, like so many that had attacked him this week, pushes forward. *Candy, in this same spot, her back against the mirror, her fingers above her head and gripping at the mirror's surface, her face filled with need, her voice begging for more. When she had come, her body had gripped him with a fierceness that had made his own release unstoppable.*

"Dinner can wait." His command, one that would have made Candy all but buck from arousal, only makes Cecile's eyes narrow.

She pushes on his chest with the hand that once held his ring. "I'm not doing this with you Nathan. You know I'm not into that dominating shit you like."

Ah yes. Another thing conveniently forgotten in her time away. Along with the memories of what a bitch she could be. His nostalgia had painted it as spirit. Two weeks of her had reminded him of why he used to work so much and play so little.

Two weeks, and she'd only recently explained her actions, saying that she'd run away out of boredom, that she hadn't felt "emotionally close enough" to him. When he'd asked her if there had been anyone else, she had only laughed. "You can't exactly play the celibate card," she'd sneered, her eyes moving to a book of Candy's that had been left behind. A book that had since disappeared, along with the closetful of clothes that Rosit Fenton had supplied. He hadn't asked where the items had gone, assuming that Cecile would need to do an emotional cleansing of sorts.

Now, it seems that he is the one who needs a cleansing. He can't so much as brush his teeth without thinking of Candy, every interaction with Cecile a constant comparison.

She moves to the closet, pushing aside hangers and examining gowns, her old items from before, all still waiting, just like him, this entire house a ridiculous shrine to a woman who feels like a stranger. What was it that he had loved about her? Where is the connection, the spark, the love that he remembers?

Maybe she had been right to leave the first time. Maybe she had seen their emotional distance and he had been blind.

She yanks a dress free and steps into it, his eyes closing, the moment too intimate for the strangers they have become.

In a moment when he finally has everything he wants, it feels like he's lost it all.

CHAPTER 51

Divorce, as it turns out, is a nasty bitch. Even with two parties willing to part ways, the dog and pony show that you perform is ridiculous. Counseling has been the biggest joke. Nathan and I both had to attend private sessions, the courts determining that two hours in the presence of a psychiatrist is enough to convince someone to change the course of their marriage's fate. I don't need a psychiatrist to convince me that I belong with Nathan. Unfortunately, that has already been decided by my stubborn mind.

Today is the required joint session—one with Dr. Bejanti, Nathan, and me. I'm sure Cecile wanted to attend, wanted to dig her manicured nails deep into Nathan's arm and hiss possessively at me, pulling up her silicone-enhanced lips to reveal razor-sharp teeth.

I have threatened, bribed, and begged my soul to not be excited, to not look forward to seeing Nathan. It is unhealthy for me to continue to want him, to continue to need his touch, his stare, that flare in his eyes that tells me he wants to fuck *now*. But my heart doesn't listen. It is pattering, it is quivering, it is jumping up and down in my chest and screaming with joy when a black Range Rover pulls up to the office and he steps out. He is effortlessly pulled together in a blue polo, worn jeans, a baseball cap pulled low over his eyes. Casual Nathan. A side I haven't often seen. A side that weighs down my pussy and causes a latent need inside of me to awaken.

His tan arms tug open the door, and suddenly he is before me, his mouth curving into a smile, his arms reaching out, pulling me to him for a hug. "Hey Candy," he whispers, and I melt against him.

It's the smell that gets me—the scent of his cologne that takes me right back to every good memory I have. Standing there, my face buried in his shirt, his arm around my waist … I can close my eyes and be back as his wife. Which is humorous, considering we are stepping into divorce counseling. The thought jolts me back to the present and I step back. "Hello Nathan."

Oh my God, my voice actually behaved. Cool and confident, it doesn't waver or squeak. I don't sound like a besotted reject or a love-struck teen. I sound … casual. Unaffected. "Where's Cecile?"

He watches me closely, unmoving, his blue eyes on mine. "The house," he says finally, and there is something in his words, but I am not savvy enough to figure them out.

I nod and sit, glancing at my watch, the Tag Heuer that I couldn't stop myself from putting on this morning.

He sits next to me, too close, the scent of him undoing me, causing my eyes to involuntarily close, my body to lean … I straighten, open my eyes, and reach for my phone, scrolling through it in an attempt to appear busy.

"How are you?" He leans in, putting his arm around the back of my chair, his fingers running gently along my arm. I start at the contact, turning to look at his hand, the strong fingers of it playing gently with my soul.

"What are you doing? Stop touching me," I snap.

He shoots me a wounded look, withdrawing his arm and checking his own watch. "Sorry," he mutters. "You don't have to act like it—"

"Mr. and Mrs. Dumont?" The man before us is Indian, short and round, with a face that beams, wire glasses tight against round cheeks.

We stand in unison, Nathan gesturing for me to go ahead, and we follow the man to his office.

It is a small office, probably designed to force the sparring couple closer, as if less space can overcome irrevocable differences. In my case, it works perfectly. Any proximity to Nathan causes me to swoon like some weak heroine in a nineteenth century romance novel.

We sit, the doctor settles in, moves some papers, and then smiles at us. "I understand we are here to discuss your marriage, and some roadblocks it may have encountered. What are the main issues in your relationship?"

Nathan casts a sidelong glance at me. "I don't know that there were any issues, per se. We separated because my ex-girlfriend returned and agreed to give our relationship another shot."

The man squints, his cheerful beam gone. "Your ex-girlfriend?"

"Well, ex-fiancée."

"And your wife presented a problem in that scenario." His inquisitive look has turned into a hard stare, full of judgment. I want to kiss the man.

"We had a marriage of convenience. Candace and I were not in love."

"Were not or are not?"

Nathan stills. "What do you mean?"

The doctor opens our file, pulling out photo upon photo and setting them on the desk before us.

Us in Seafire, bent over lobster, my hand clasped in his.
On the beach, his head bent to mine, our bodies molded as one.
A close up of his face, beaming at me, wind whipping our hair.

Paparazzi photos cut from some magazine. A coordinated image created by lies.

"These photos indicate a couple very much in love."

"It was fake," I interrupt whatever bullshit Nathan is about to say. "We pretended. In hopes that Nathan's ex-fiancée would see."

"Hmm …" The man seems unconvinced, leaning back in his chair and staring at us. "Tell me more about this marriage of convenience. What was the point?"

"My attorney has informed me that there is no legal standing that a couple must wed for reasons of love—" Nathan's curt sentence is ended by Dr. Bejanti's irritable expression, waving his hand dismissively.

"I don't care about the law. I only care about the two of you. Why did you get married?"

"For her." *Shit, there was some bitterness in my tone.* They both notice it and look at me simultaneously.

The doctor frowns. "It was all a ploy to entice jealousy? Marriage is a bit dramatic, don't you think?"

Nathan shrugs. "I dated around a lot in the first few years after she left me. She, and the press, didn't find that very exciting. Plus…" He glances at me. "Candace understood the limitations of our relationship."

I want to get the *fuck* out of here. Listening to him speak, listening to our fucked up marriage being analyzed … It makes me sound pathetic, reminds me of how our entire relationship was centered on *her.* I feel a wave of physical nausea, thinking of her in the car, Nathan and I doing a coordinated dance so that we can be divorced and she and him can be together.

"Are you going to marry her?" The question pops out of me suddenly. Nathan's eyes sharpen, a question in them.

I straighten, meeting his eyes. "Are you? Are you planning to marry her?"

"I don't think so," he says slowly. "We're still … working through a few things."

I pin my lips together, and hope the irritation doesn't show on my face. "Just wondering."

He tilts his head, frowning, light flickering in those baby blues. "Do you—I mean…" He pauses to collect his thoughts. "Would it *bother* you if we married?"

I want to strangle the man, wrap my hands around that sexy neck and squeeze some sense into him. "No," I say quietly, meeting his eyes. "I was just wondering."

We stare at each other for a long moment, my heart fighting to stay composed. Then he leans forward swiftly, grabbing the back of my neck, and kisses me.

CHAPTER 52

Damn. I never could hide from his kiss. And the communication line between us hasn't lost any of its strength during our time apart. He doesn't hesitate, doesn't ask my permission before pressing his lips to mine, my mouth opening instantly, my hands reaching up and gripping his shirt, twisting the cotton with need, my desire to touch any and every part of him overriding my attempt to be passive.

Everything I feel, everything I miss, goes into that kiss. I tell my story of heartbreak and need and desire with my tongue, with my begging strokes and carnal swipes. And his mouth speaks with possessive, aggressive movement, his breath ragged, his mouth taking mine and reclaiming what was once his.

A woman's desperation is most clearly spoken in a kiss. And I'm afraid, in this moment, that I bare my soul to him. Everything that I have contained, held back, lied to myself about, comes to the surface, all of my emotions revealed at once, both to me and to him.

I can't take it, can't take the memory of his touch reawakening. I can't take my feelings laid out, naked before this man. I push on his shirt, breaking the connection of our lips, pressing hard with my fists until we are fully separated, his eyes tight on mine, desperation in their midst.

He stares at me, his chest moving beneath my hands, his eyes almost accusatory in their intensity and dismay. "Candy," he whispers, sliding his hand around and cupping my neck. "I had no idea …"

I push, ripping myself from the seat and the burn of his hands, grabbing my purse and running for the door, passing through hallways and lobbies. I don't stop and compose myself, don't listen when the receptionist calls out my name. I have one focus, and I zero in on it. Get the fuck out of here and into the safety of my car.

Damn the payment for our session.

Damn the blonde bitch in *my* house.
Damn Nathan and his fucking kiss.
Damn the doctor with his questions and how he will react to what just happened.

I don't stop until I am several miles away, jerking the wheel sideways and bringing the car to a quick, shuddering stop in an abandoned strip mall. There, I shift into park, drop my head to the steering wheel, and cry.

I can't do it. I can't sit across from him and sign a document that will dissolve our marriage. I can't see the two of them together, can't see the look on his face when he stares into her eyes. I will physically break in half if I see them kiss, or see her smile, or if they embrace once the verdict is rendered. This should have been easy: a sterile environment with a doctor, a few easy questions, and we part. How did something so simple turn into something so terrible?

Now he knows. He knows how I feel. He knows that while he was acting, I was sincere. He knows that I am weak and vulnerable, and that he has hurt me. Everything I have fought so hard to project— my cool, confident demeanor—just crashed and burned in that cramped office. Now he knows the truth. And I look the fool.

CHAPTER 53

A year ago, I would have cringed at a call from my bank, my account most likely overdrawn, NSF fees pending. Now, the number displays and I feel only guilt. I rise from my chair and quietly move from my father's room, answering the call once I am in the hall.

"Is this Mrs. Dumont?" The crisp voice doesn't know how the name hits my ears, how it is both a knife and a salve to my heart.

"Yes." I should change my name back, after the divorce, but I don't know that I will. I'm not yet ready to separate from the one thing that made me his wife.

"We need to talk about the balance in your account."

"Is there a problem?" There shouldn't be, but my heart still quickens, our Nassau actions illegal, despite the solid intentions behind them.

"Not exactly…" the man pauses. "It's just uncommon for so much money to sit in a savings account. The rate of interest is so nominal. Can you come in, and we can discuss a money market, or CD? Something more appropriate for those funds."

I can't put the money in a CD. I can't tie it up, not when every bone in my body is screaming at me to give it back. Four point five million dollars, that's what this man is going on about. Four point five million dollars of Nathan's money, that I stole.

You see, researching Cecile wasn't the only thing I did at the library that day. I also took my passport and the piece of paper Drew had given me, with Candace's social security number and the account number written neatly on its front.

And there, from a courtesy phone in the library's lobby, with a prepaid long-distance calling card and list of Bahamian banks, I called each one, until I found the one with an account in my name. And then, that day before our flight, I transferred some of the funds out of CeeCee's account.

I didn't take much, though *much* is such a relative term. It wasn't much when you looked at the balance in the account, but it was a massive infusion to my old bank account—an account that had never carried a balance of more than a thousand dollars.

Four and a half million—approximately half the interest that had accumulated in the account in the four years since Nathan's big deposit. Despite the appearance to Nathan, the account *had* earned a healthy rate of return, allowing me to siphon off a large chunk without tipping him off.

Mr. Brantling was correct; the transfer was easily done by phone. I downloaded the appropriate forms, scanned in a copy of my passport, and had the item notarized by the library's receptionist. Fuck saving fifteen percent on car insurance in fifteen minutes. I became a millionaire in half that time.

It had been an insurance policy. I had Nathan's word that he would take care of my father. His word, and a contract that was, at best, questionably enforceable. I'd needed to protect myself, needed a parachute in case I got ripped from the Dumont luxury jet. I'd gotten a brief window of opportunity, and I'd had to decide in that split second if I would take the opportunity or let it pass. Poor planning had always been my downfall. That one, single moment, I'd wanted to make the right decision, to do something that would turn my life in the correct direction, for my father and me. I could always give the money back if things went right and Nathan kept his word. But I would never be able to recreate that opportunity. I would never have that chance again.

So I took it. I took it, and then Nathan kept his word, and now I'm stuck with all of it, and the uncertain footing of what to do with it.

"Please move it to a money market account," I say quietly. "It can stay there."

The man launches into questions and address confirmations, credit card offers and emergency lines of credit. It's funny. The more money you have, the more they want to give. I walk down the hall to the kitchen, propping the phone against my shoulder as I reach for a cup.

It's been two weeks since our session with the counselor, and I don't need his fancy degree or assessment to know that I might never heal from Nathan. I have buried myself in activity, in an insane hope that I might escape his memory by spending money, doing crosswords, and searching for a job.

I pour coffee into the cup, glancing at the granite countertops and thinking of my own new kitchen, in the apartment I have leased, thirty minutes outside of Nashville, in a beautiful area closer to Dad. I left my old life in that Destin storage unit, where it will probably sit for a decade. I want to start fresh, to erase any memory of my time at Sammy's, and—hopefully—my time with Nathan.

His money makes that hard. I can't help but be grateful every time I swipe my debit card, walk through my well-appointed home, or open the door to my Mercedes.

Once I get a job, I'll probably pay it all back, send him a giant check for all of it. Probably. I'm not altruistic enough to commit to that just yet. There is the matter of my broken heart, and what that is worth in severance pay.

I haven't heard a word from him since our kiss at Dr. Bejanti's office. No letter from Mark regarding the divorce, no call from his attorney. I've stopped looking at the gossip magazines, forbid myself to Google his name or scroll through the internet for pictures of them together. It is too painful to see them, too hurtful to know that they are happy and I am miserable.

I half-expect another psychiatry session to be required, given the disastrous conclusion of our group session. But no one has called, and nothing has come by mail. Something will soon. Our marriage's death is imminent.

Dad is doing great. They have discovered his ailment, a rare blood disease that was killing his immune system and affecting his body's ability to heal. There is a treatment, and he is in the first round of the new medication. Just this morning I reserved an apartment for him on the ground floor of my building. It seems a little premature, and I worry about jinxing his progress, but I want to be ready when he is released. This apartment will allow him to be independent, yet still close to me. Pam has already set me up with an at-home nurse, one who can help him once he leaves Crestridge.

Today is a quiet day. Dad has slept most of the morning, and I have read. It's lasagna day in the cafeteria, and I am watching the clock for 11:30 a.m., which is the earliest time I can get a plate.

I end the call and return to his room, settling into the recliner, my coffee set on the table, my legs curling underneath me. I close my eyes. Just a quick nap, long enough to tide me the twenty-two minutes until lasagna time.

***

I drive, taking the long way home, through the hills, rolling down the windows so that the smell of fall and foliage fills my car. Then I slow, turning into my complex, coming to a sudden and sharp stop when I see the black Range Rover parked in front of my apartment, and the man that is leaning against its hood.

I stare at him through the windshield, watching as he straightens, looking at me, our eyes catching over fifty feet of broken blacktop. My foot wavers on the brake, my brain arguing with my heart, arguing with my instinct, my foot caught in a tug-of-war between the two. I put it out of its misery and put the car into park, opening the door and getting out in the middle of the lot.

He is so handsome it should be a sin. Standing tall, his hair messy, a loosened tie gaping over a white shirt and dark dress pants, his tan skin pulls the entire look together too effortlessly. His stature and manner reek of the casual perfection brought on by decades of wealth and breeding. He moves away from the car, stepping toward me, and I hold up a shaky hand. "Stop."

I cannot take him any closer. Cannot have those lips coming into focus, not now that I know what they can do to me. Tearing down my walls and invading my heart, they will leave me gasping, tearful, and alone, while he returns to her. "What are you doing here, Nathan?"

He shoves his hands into his pockets, and stops, tilting his head. "I need to speak to you." His voice grumbles, a gravelly, deep sound that makes me wet and has me clenching my hands into fists to keep from reaching out for him.

"Why?"

He steps forward, closer, his eyes on mine, everything else disappearing as he closes the gap and draws me in. I inhale sharply, his scent reaching me, my willpower eroding with every inch that I lose as he steps nearer. I am too weak. I cannot take another touch, another breath of him. I will break.

"I left her," he says, stopping before me, his gentle hand grabbing my chin before it drops and pulling it back up, his blue eyes seducing me with their initial contact.

I frown, trying to make sense of his words. "Cecile? Why?"

"I didn't want to do to her what I did to you."

I narrow my eyes, stepping back, my elbow catching the side mirror of the car, causing a sharp spike of pain. "What? Fuck her and then send her to her room?"

He winces, his blue eyes clouding. "No. Be with her when I am in love with someone else." He steps closer, his hands pushing my waist until I am against the car, my body responding, curving when he leans forward, pinning me with his body, the heat of his muscles hard against my frame.

I can't breathe, the weight of his words too heavy against my chest. What I want to believe is too risky—I cannot take my heart down that path if I am wrong. It is too cruel, too much for its fragile existence to take. "What do you mean?" I whisper.

"I love you, Candy. I love you with every fiber of my being, every beat of my heart. I can't stay away from you. I can't live without seeing your smile or hearing your voice."

I shake my head, pushing against his chest. "Bullshit, Nathan. You were consumed with *her*. *She* was the love of your life!"

"No." he whispers, staring at my face. "No. I wanted the unattainable because it was unattainable. I remembered all of the good and forgot the bad. When we were apart, those four years I spent searching for her … we both changed during that time, became different people.

The woman I thought I loved … that isn't her. And if that is, then maybe now I just realize there is something better out there." He swallows, the movement making his jaw clench, something akin to vulnerability in his eyes. "You."

I shake my head before he even finishes, trying to clear the cobwebs and find rational thought somewhere inside. I cannot fall for this; I cannot accept his smooth words and romantic notions. I am not the desperate stripper who he met that night. I do not suck dick for money or need a knight in shining armor. I deserve someone who wants to be with me, not someone who wants what they can't have.

"You said you wanted the unattainable because it was unattainable. I am now that unattainable property, and you just want—"

He kisses me, crushing my moving lips with his own, his hands fisting into my hair, his leg working in between mine, the full length of his body hard against my own. His hands pull my mouth tight to his, not asking, but taking my soul, his tongue claiming me, tasting my resistance as his mouth feasts on me. He speaks between frantic kisses. "I need you … to breathe. It's more … so much more than I ever had with her." Somewhere, a car honks, the wind picks up my hair and blows it into the air, and I lose my resolve, softening against his body, my hands crawling up his back and clawing at his shirt. I yield easily when he lifts me, sets me on the warm hood, his head dipping down and planting frantic kisses on my neck, my chest, up the line of my jaw, his hands gripping my ass and pulling me to the edge, until his hard body is flush against me.

The time without him has been so long, my body craving him in a way that is almost painful, and I gasp when he presses against me, my body so sensitive and yearning for fulfillment. "Take me inside," I pant. "Now."

CHAPTER 54

He takes my key fob, promising to park the car, and I fly up the exterior staircase, fumbling with my keys until the door is unlocked, and I am inside, my jacket flying off, tennis shoes and jeans being yanked off as I move. My mind is frantically trying to slow my body, throwing words of reason at me as I move, but my lust has taken over. I need him inside of me *now*, and will deal with the aftermath later.

My shirt is halfway over my head when I hear the door bang open, steps moving across tile, and then his hands are helping me. My head is suddenly free, and his mouth on mine.

God, I love this man. The way he touches me, the way he kisses me. The cuts of his body and the intensity of his eyes. He is a drug that I have no way of resisting, bad for my soul, but so heartbreakingly perfect in its deliverance.

He lifts me, my legs wrapping around his waist, my hands working at the buttons of his shirt, yanking his tie over his head and then reclaiming his mouth. He lays me on the kitchen island, the open surface cold on my skin, his body shifting down, until the heat of his mouth is on my stomach, and his hands are skimming my panties down and off my body.

I haven't shaved and try to push him off, my feet finding and pressing on his shoulders. He knocks them aside, spreading my legs and focusing on my pussy, his eyes glancing up to meet mine.

Damn. Just the look in them knocks me backward—so full of raw, uncontrollable lust. He breathes hard, staring at me before looking back down, his fingers opening me up before his eyes. "God, you have no idea how beautiful you are. Your lips, your pink center. There is nothing hotter, nothing more beautiful than this right here." He groans, lowering his mouth, swiping a hot tongue down my open slit, his tongue tickling the skin, making me moan and spread wider, moisture dripping down the crack of my ass, my need for him so great. "You taste so good," he whispers, as his tongue flicks over the wet knot of my clit. The intensity of the contact is so strong that I moan, arching into his mouth, his hands slipping under and gripping the checks of my ass, pulling me into his mouth.

He buries his face into my pussy, his mouth hot and wet, his gentle strums across the sensitive bud making me squirm. I prop up on my elbows, watching him, the view so carnal, so fucking hot. His face between my trembling thighs, blue eyes fixed on mine as he sucks and flicks my clit to perfection. There's the strong arc of his shoulders, the strength of his hands, squeezing my ass as he worships my body. I am close, my body trembling beneath his mouth, when he slides one hand lower, pressing on the pucker of my ass, borrowing moisture from my center, and dipping inside of that hot, tight hole.

It pushes me over the edge and I cry out, the orgasm blinding in its intensity, my eyes squeezing shut, his finger tight inside of me, his tongue stretching the orgasm further, knowing instinctively when to soften, how to prolong the waves of pleasure.

I don't know when he pulls out, when his mouth leaves me. I am a mess of post-coital languish, stretched out on the counter, the island the perfect width for my stretched-out form. I feel my legs as they are moved, hear his voice as he moves around me, and feel him slide me off the surface and into his arms.

The bed. Soft beneath me, his naked weight above me, he spreads my legs with his knees. He is glorious—his body so perfect, the length of his shaft so virile, my cave-woman impulses in full force.

I see man.
I need man.
I want man to make me fucking his.

He strokes his cock, putting a finger in, testing my readiness, his eyes hardening at the touch. "Jesus, Candy. You are so ready for me."

I don't respond, my heart finding nothing to say. I *am* ready for him. I have been ready for him since the moment he walked into Sammy's. I am just ready for so much more than he can give me.

Then, he presses the stiff head of his cock against my slit, and any logical thought goes out the window. At this moment, everything my body needs, he is about to provide.

I am as tight as the first night he fucked me, and he swears as he slides his cock all the way in, so deep that I gasp. "You are so tight," he groans, leaning forward, my legs wrapping around him. "You haven't …" His eyes ask me the question, and I shake my head, biting my bottom lip. "Fuck," he swears, lowering his mouth to mine, his elbows framing my head, his mouth taking me in and stealing my heart.

He pauses, his head lifting, our kiss broken, and there is one quiet moment where he only looks into my eyes. "I love you," he whispers. "I'm sorry. You deserve so much better than what I gave you."

When he thrusts forward with his hips, it is slow, his muscular thighs trembling, and I yelp from the satisfaction, both of my body, and my heart. "I will treasure you," he says, the words thick with emotion, every drag of his manhood a new lesson in pleasure.

"You better," I breath, and his eyes light with a smile.

"I will earn your love," he promises, sliding down slightly, the angle changing, his hands cupping and squeezing my breasts together, his rough thumbs rubbing over my nipples. "I have spent every day thinking about your smile, your heart. I've cursed myself for everything that I don't know about you, and for all of the moments I've missed."

His fingers bite into my skin and his eyes change, that predatory arousal taking over them. "And I have spent every night thinking about your body, every night picturing you stretched across my bed. I miss your mouth on my cock, miss your sweet ass bent over before me, in sore need of a fucking spanking." The last words are ripped from his mouth, and he moves higher, thrusting hard, the firm length of him burying inside of me. I moan, begging him for more, and feel him respond, twitching inside of me, his strokes quickening.

"I love your bare cock inside of me," I moan, wrapping my hands around his neck and pulling his mouth to my tits, his eager response lighting a flame to my arousal, my core tightening around his cock. "I love how hard you fuck me, like you have to get every inch inside of me, like you will never get enough."

"I won't," he grounds out, lifting from my breasts. "I will never get enough of you. It's not just this. I need all of you. In bed and out. I want to wake up next to you every fucking day. I want to have babies with you and watch them grow up. I want … I just—"

As much as I want to hear his words, I can't hold back the orgasm that rips through me, my body bucking beneath his, my panicked eyes meeting his, a look that he instantly understands.

And fuck, he knows exactly what to do. Drilling me hard and fast, my head dropping back, breasts shaking as he gives me every inch of him, his slick, hard cock so thick, so perfect, so animalistic in its possessiveness. We are animals, broken down to our core needs; I am his mark, and he is feasting. As I come apart, as my orgasm shakes me down to the soul, as I experience the true, piercing pleasure that breaks me down to nothing, I know only one thing: I will never be able to resist this man. Not his body, and not his heart. I am his, to do with as he wishes.

CHAPTER 55

ONE YEAR LATER

He will be home soon. The gates will open, his car will turn down the drive, and then he will be here. Just like every day, except that today I tell him my secret.

Three months ago, we signed a new document—one that nullified any prior document and prenuptial agreement of any kind. If we separate, I am entitled to half of everything. I no longer need my safety net—the millions that are still tucked away in my checking account. The money has been like a virus, eating away at my otherwise perfect life. I need an antidote. I need to be cleansed.

I should have told him already. But everything has been so perfect. It is as if the man I was with before was preoccupied, and now he is free. Focused. On our life together. There are no rules; there are no secrets, except for mine.

The first few weeks we dealt with Cecile, her calls, her attempts to stop by the house. Drew is the one who finally controlled her, in his final task as Nathan's employee. I think he has rejoined the police force, and I heard Cecile has moved to Paris. There has been no word from their camps in almost ten months, a silence I am grateful for.

I sit by the pool, my face turned to the sun, and wait, the soft pants of Groucho, our Lab, beside me. My eyes drift over to the guesthouse. What was once my home has been redone. It is now my office. The trophy wives of our expensive corner of the world now come to me for their parties, their teas, and their eight-year-old's lavish birthday parties. The bed was taken out, a large worktable put in its place. The walls are now covered with idea boards, the bookshelves full of magazines and scrapbooks. I am not the local's first choice for weddings and charity galas, but events too small to be dealt with by the big planners—those are my bread and butter. It keeps me busy, and I love the work, gaining confidence and experience with each event.

I am officially a wife. No longer just in name, but also in action. The stoic, cold man who I once knew is now a sexy, playful man who spoils me rotten and tells me every night how much I mean to him. Then he typically throws me on the bed and rocks my sexual world. He tapes love notes to the mirror, wakes me up with kisses and soft caresses, and has completely won my father's heart, becoming close friends with the old man who once only knew him through photos. My father is now well, on daily medication, but living a normal life. He has a place in town, fifteen minutes away, and is a frequent guest in our home.

I look down at my hands, at the check that lies there.

$4,500,000.00. Cashing this check will leave a balance of just over fifteen thousand, enough to pay off the remaining student loans and credit cards that I have lingering about.

It will be a weight off my shoulders, giving it back, even though I am on his accounts now, and know the full extent of his wealth. This money is not needed; it will be excess cream on an already overflowing cup. But for me, the act is symbolic. I am giving him my trust. Destroying my safety net. Putting my faith in him—in us.

The check won't fix everything. At moments when he is being especially sweet, when his eyes are full of love and shining at me like I can do no wrong ... I think about Drew. Even though it meant nothing, even though I was filling a hole that Nathan had dug, it sits there, on my conscience. I keep waiting, thinking that he will bring it back up, will ask more questions. But maybe he feels about Drew the same way that I feel about Cecile. I don't want to hear about anything they did, or words that passed between them. I only want to know that his heart is mine, and that he wants nothing to do with her.

My hands fist nervously around the check, wondering at his reaction to it. I know that he loves me. Loves me in a way stronger than he ever felt for Cecile. It took a while for me to fully grasp and accept that. For me, I think I always knew how I felt. I was lost to him the moment I saw him, the moment his eyes followed me in the dark club. I was always his, and I finally believe that he is fully mine. To have. To hold. Till death do us part.

I hear the drag of gates, the crunch of tires, and know that he is here. Gripping the check, I stand and move to meet my husband.

*****

He greets me with an easy smile, tossing a set of plans onto the side table and sweeping me into his arms. His hand gathers my hair, tenderly gripping it as his mouth takes my own, his free arm curving around and pulling me tightly into him.

I push gently against his chest, the hand holding the check squished between our bodies. "I need to talk to you."

His eyes turn serious, his hand stilling on my hair. "What's wrong? Is it your father?"

I shake my head quickly. "No, nothing's wrong. I just need a minute with you."

He tilts his head, a question in his eyes, and smiles warily. "Okay. Let's go to the couch."

He settles into the leather, looking at me expectantly. I sit on the ottoman before him, my hand gripping the folded check tightly. "There's something I haven't been honest about. Something I did a long time ago." I hold out the check and he takes it, unfolding it slowly, his eyes scanning the paper's surface before he looks up at me. He raises his eyebrows, waiting for me to explain. "I ... When I found out about the money, the Bahamas ... I thought you might leave me." I pause, tucking my hair behind my ear. "I thought you'd want me to leave once you got the money, once I fulfilled my purpose. With my father, with his medical bills ... I took some of the money. As a safety net. From CeeCee's account."

He glances down at the check. "A four and a half million dollar safety net?" His voice is quiet, scarily so, devoid of any emotion, no clues in his tone.

I shrug weakly, panic increasing at his lack of reaction. "I'm sorry Nathan. I just couldn't imagine Cecile *not* coming back. And I saw how much you loved her. I knew that I would lose that battle—that you would leave me and choose her. I could afford to disappoint myself, but I couldn't re-abandon my father."

He leans forward and gently lifts my chin, pulling my eyes to his. "I didn't love her," he says firmly. "I thought I did. But what we have? *This* is love." He holds my gaze until I nod, then releases me, sitting back and looking at the check, his face tight. "Your father's situation doesn't excuse what you did."

I swallow hard, my heart rate increasing. I had expected Nathan to be angry, had prepared myself for an argument, a practiced apology ready. But I didn't expect, hadn't prepared myself for any *serious* consequences. Not from the man who had proven day after day, in every moment of the last year, that he was head over heels in love with me. But now, looking at his tight face and hearing the granite in his words, the gravity of this situation hits me full force. I'd *stolen* millions of dollars from him. I'd kept a secret of enormous magnitude through a year's worth of "I love you's" and early morning cuddles. This is a sin that could cause our demise. I had flippantly expected forgiveness, never thinking of the horrific alternative.

He clears his throat. "But, neither did my situation excuse my behavior." I blink at him, trying to understand his statement, my mind stuttering back and piecing his sentences together.

He leans forward, pulling me off the ottoman and onto his lap, cradling me in his arms, my head in the crook of his arm, looking up and into that gorgeous, impossibly perfect face. He furrows his brow, his finger tracing the line of my mouth as he speaks. "I did a lot of things during our first time together that I am ashamed of. You had every reason to hate me during that time. We, despite what was on paper, were not husband and wife. I was in no way, shape, or form, worthy of being called your husband. I wouldn't blame you for anything you did during that time, especially if it brought you peace of mind or security." He bends down, brushing his lips over mine. Then he pulls away, a smile tugging at his mouth. He taps the check gently on my chest. "This money?" He drops the paper, letting it fall gently on my shirt. "I always knew, Candy. CeeCee's statements have come to this address since the day I opened that account for her. I've known the balance of that account to the penny and watched it grow."

It takes me a moment to understand. "What? You've known this whole time?"

He grins, sliding his hand under the bottom hem of my shirt, his warm palm tickling my skin as he gently rubs his thumb over the planes of my stomach. "Yes, my devious, sexy wife. I knew."

"Why didn't you say something? Weren't you mad?" He slides his hand downward, the tips of his fingers slipping under my shorts and trailing the lace of my panties. His expression sobers, his eyes locking on mine. "At the time, I thought it was a good sign—proof that you wouldn't take it all and run. Proof that you would follow through and help me out."

I frown, my mind traveling back over the events of our parting. "If you knew I had all this money, why did you still pay for my father?"

"It was ego. I couldn't bear you thinking that you were right—that I was an asshole who would abandon you as soon as my ex-girlfriend showed up." His playful grin drops, intensity coming into his eyes. "The Bahamas was the first time you looked at me as if you cared. As if I was worth more than sex. That look stuck with me. I was holding out hope that I might see it again."

Relief floods me, stress leaving my body at his words. I close my eyes as he undoes my shorts, his hand stealing deeper, further into the lace boundary of my sex. "So ... I'm forgiven?" I mumble, catching my breath when his fingers climb deftly lower, his hand cupping me as his fingers push the fabric of my panties against and slightly inside of my wet core.

His mouth moves to mine. "If you can forgive the ass that I was, I can forgive anything and everything you choose to torture me with over the next lifetime."

"Torture, huh?" I smile against his mouth, pulling away from his kiss long enough to stand, sliding my shorts over my hips and dropping them to the floor.

"You have something in mind?" he growls.

"Sit back, Mr. Dumont." I kneel before him, running my hands firmly up the thighs of his suit and over the outline of his cock, unbuckling his belt and tugging on the zipper. "Torture is an art I have mastered."

He inhales when I slide my hands inside, his hard skin hot against my palm. "God, I love you."

And then, our relationship continues the way it began, with me on my knees, his hard cock in my hand. But other than the wetness between my thighs, and the dominating sexuality of his too-gorgeous-for-words presence, everything else has changed.

I've gotten my happily ever after. Nathan was my golden ticket to the good life, and—much more importantly—true love and genuine happiness. If I weren't throat-deep in delicious cock, I would pinch myself.

EPILOGUE

FIVE YEARS LATER

"No." Her eyes flash at him, the stubbornness causing him to laugh. "I will *not* put my pants on."

"You have to put your pants on." I interrupt, snagging the back of her shirt and pulling her toward me. "Grandpa is going to be here in less than ten minutes to take you to the park and the park requires little girls to wear pants."

"It *is* a stupid rule," Nathan comments, holding out the hot purple jeans, which Bella snatches at with a frown. She sits down, holding out her chubby feet, which I brush off before working the pants on, my eyes catching the look that Nathan gives the two of us, a tender one that fills me with happiness.

Once properly attired, I shoo her off to the porch, the click of her shoes followed by Groucho. Nathan stands, and I hold up my hands to him. "Help me up, my love."

He pulls me to my feet and against his chest, taking a gentle nip of my neck before releasing him. "How long will this park event take?" he inquires, his hands sliding underneath my T-shirt, his thumbs working their way under my sports bra.

I giggle, tugging at the top of his jeans. "I told Dad to keep her for at least two hours, and to call on the way back."

"Two hours?" he narrows his eyes. "Two hours isn't long enough to defile every surface in this house."

"Well you shouldn't have such a big house, Mr. Dumont," I chide.

"We shouldn't?" He questions. "I thought you wanted to fill up those other rooms with babies."

"I don't know," I muse, running my hands through his hair. "I'm not sure that life can get any more perfect than this."

Fifteen minutes later, as my dad's truck carries Bella past our front gates, I eat my words. Nathan lifts me onto the dining room table, and everything crystallizes in the moment he pushes inside of me. It turns out, life can get about nine inches better. I tell him so, and a grin interrupts the canvas of his fierce sexuality.

"I love you," he says gruffly, his mouth lowering to mine, his movements slowing as he takes his time with the kiss.

"I love you too." I wrap my arms around his neck, arching into his body, my breasts against his bare chest.

He growls out my name, twisting my hair in his hands, and when I wrap my legs around his waist, both of us get lost in the pleasure.

Our words stop.
Our skin slaps.
His breath pants.
My heart thuds.

The first orgasm rips, and in it, I lose any last bit of restraint. I embrace the father of my child, the provider of my life, the deliverer of my pleasure, the owner of my heart. I cry out his name and meet his eyes, the connection one thick with need and passion and love.

I will have him as long as there is breath in our bodies.

I will hold him as long as there is strength in our arms.

"Till death" does not apply to us. We will live on in the afterlife, in next lives or heavenly places.

We will never part. I know it as certainly as my next words.

"Nathan?"

"What?"

"Fuck me harder." I smile. "Now."

Note from the Author

Candy and Nathan have been a part of my life since 2013, when I first wrote, and released, their story as a series of novellas. I published them as I wrote them, which meant that I didn't alway plan properly for latter events to unfold. It causes a rougher experience for the reader, and this story has been a bit of a stick in my side for the past four years. I've always vowed to return to this couple, and when a window of time appeared, I grabbed it and dove back into their world.

Whew, what a sexy world it is! I had so much fun reacquainting myself with Drew, Nathan and Candy. I realized early on that I needed to add some of Nathan's point of view, to show his side of things. And I improved a bit on Candy, making her a stronger heroine, despite the situation she's gotten herself into. :)

If you are an original reader from the days of the novellas, or are new to this couple—I hope you enjoyed their story. If you are looking for a similar read of mine, you will probably like Sex Love Repeat.

Also, if you've ever thought about writing a novel yourself, you may be interested in Alessandra Torre Ink, or my How to Write Your First Book course! You can check out both of those items at www.alessandratorreink.com.

Thank you so much to Perla Calas, my proofreader and editor on this novel. Thank you to Tricia Crouch, my PA and right arm. A giant grateful hug to Natasha is a Book Junkie, for her insights and suggestions - you saved Nathan from a thousand reader glares. And thank you to The Next Step PR, for your publicity of this novel. More thanks goes to SueBee, the incredible Shhluts, my amazing Torreville ladies, the ARC Addicts, Erik Gevers, Judi Perkins, Lauren Perry, and all of the readers and authors who helped to spread the word about this novel. I couldn't be successful with out every one of you.

If you'd like to be notified when my next book releases, or to sign up for my popular monthly newsletter, please go to www.nextnovel.com.

xoxo,

Alessandra Torre